Dear Reader:

In a previous life, before the time of Plum, I wrote twelve short romance novels. Red-hot screwball comedies, each and every one of them. Nine of these stories were originally published by the Loveswept line between the years 1988 and 1992. All went out of print immediately and could be found only at used bookstores and yard sales.

I'm excited to tell you that those nine stories (plus one from the Second Chance at Love line) have been re-released by HarperCollins. *The Grand Finale* was the very first Loveswept published and is now the last to be reprinted. It's presented here in close to original form. I've done some editing to improve readability and wardrobe.

The Grand Finale is the story of a young woman who falls out of a tree, onto a pizza, and into love. Okay, so maybe the road to true love isn't all that easy. Truth is, she ruins the pizza, loses three cars, adopts three little old ladies, is held at gunpoint, and is caught ogling a very hot, very gorgeous, almost naked guy. Happily, she eventually gets to see the hot guy *entirely* naked, and they make some really great pizza together.

Enjoy!

Janet Evanovich

> *Berry blinked at the hunk of masculinity that bent over her. "Am I dead?"*

"Not yet."

"I feel dead. I must be bleeding. My back is all warm and sticky."

He squatted beside her and looked more closely. "I don't see any blood, just some pizza sauce oozing through this crumpled box. Lady, you've squished this poor pizza to smithereens." He extracted the pizza box. "Is this mine?"

Berry nodded. She was relieved to find that he was fully clothed in a pair of jeans and a navy hooded sweatshirt. She made an attempt to sit up and began a methodical check of any bones that might be broken.

"What happened? I heard something crashing around out here, and there you were . . . lying on my pizza. Are you okay?" He picked bits of bark from her tangled hair. He glanced at the profusion of broken branches scattered on the ground and understanding flickered behind observant eyes. His attention turned to the tree, traveling up the height of it, resting on the large limb just outside his bedroom window. Incredulity registered on his face. "Lady, you must be kidding! You can't be that hard up to see a naked man."

Berry blushed clear to the roots of her hair . . .

Books by Janet Evanovich

Motor Mouth • *Metro Girl*

Foul Play • *Naughty Neighbor* • *Wife for Hire*

The Grand Finale • *Thanksgiving* • *Smitten*
Manhunt • *Back to the Bedroom*
Love Overboard • *The Rocky Road to Romance*

One for the Money • *Two for the Dough*
Three to Get Deadly • *Four to Score* • *High Five*
Hot Six • *Seven Up* • *Hard Eight*
Visions of Sugar Plums • *To the Nines*
Ten Big Ones • *Eleven on Top*
Twelve Sharp • *Plum Lovin'*
Lean Mean Thirteen • *Plum Lucky*
Fearless Fourteen

JANET EVANOVICH

The Grand Finale

HARPER

An Imprint of HarperCollinsPublishers

This book was originally published as a Loveswept paperback in 1988, in a slightly altered form, by Bantam Books, a division of Bantam Dell Publishing Group, Inc.

HARPER

An Imprint of HarperCollins*Publishers*
10 East 53rd Street
New York, New York 10022-5299

Copyright © 1988 by Janet Evanovich; 2009 by Evanovich, Inc.
Back cover author photo by Deborah Feingold Photography
ISBN 978-0-06-059875-4

First Harper paperback printing: March 2009

HarperCollins ® and Harper ® are registered trademarks of Harper-Collins Publishers.

Printed in the United States of America

Visit Harper paperbacks on the World Wide Web at
www.harpercollins.com

10 9 8 7 6 5 4 3 2 1

Chapter 1

Berry Knudsen eased her battered army surplus Jeep over to the curb, pulled the emergency brake on, and studied the only mailbox in the deserted cul-de-sac. No name. No street number. Terrific. She squinted into the blackness and reread the address taped to the large pizza box on the seat next to her. 5077 Ellenburg Drive. This had to be it. This was Ellenburg Drive, and this was the only house for a quarter of a mile. She thunked her forehead onto the steering wheel and groaned. Last delivery of the night, and it had all the earmarks of a prank.

The house was a three-story Victorian perched on a small hillock. A sliver of moon ducked behind the clouds throwing ghostly highlights over the house, and a chill March wind moaned through a giant oak standing guard over the lawn on the south side. Berry grimaced and decided Jack the Ripper would have felt comfy here. Quasimodo could have added a bell tower and been happy as a clam at high tide. And Count Dracula would have traded half the blood in Transylvania for a house like this. But it's not in Transylvania, Berry reminded herself. It's in suburban Seattle and probably belongs to some nice little old lady and her nephew . . . Norman Bates.

She grimly noted that there wasn't a light shining anywhere. No car in the driveway. No sign of life that might require a large pizza with the works. Damn. She really should go up and ring the doorbell. How bad could the thing lurking behind the ornate, hand-carved front door be? Probably just some hungry pervert, sitting in the dark in his boxers, waiting for the pizza delivery lady.

Berry pushed her short blond curls behind her ear. She was being ridiculous. How did she come up with these ideas? Mr. Large Pizza with the Works simply wasn't home. He probably went out for a six-pack of beer and maybe a hatchet. Happened all the time. And since he wasn't home, there certainly wasn't any reason that she should go up and ring the doorbell. What she should do was get her keister the heck out of this creepy cul-de-sac.

A cat cried in the distance, and the hairs on Berry's neck stood on end. Beads of sweat popped out on her upper lip. She held the steering wheel in a death grip, and the pathetic little meow, filled with fear and wavering uncertainty, echoed through the still air again. Berry closed her eyes and slumped in her seat. It was worse than a cat. It was the cry of a kitten. She was doomed. She was a sucker for lost dogs, fallen nestlings, and stranded kittens. It called out again into the darkness, and Berry grabbed the pizza box and set off across the lawn, drawing courage from the fact that the Victorian house looked less sinister at close range. It had been freshly painted lemon yellow. The intricate gingerbread trim sported a new coat of white. The windows were curtainless, but the panes reflected a recent cleaning. The cat looked down at Berry from a tall oak tree and swished its tail.

"Kitty, kitty, kitty," Berry called softly.

Meow.

Berry bit her lower lip. The dumb cat was stuck in the tree. A blast of wind ruffled the kitten's fur, causing the little ball of fluff to huddle closer to the limb. Berry rolled her eyes and plunked the pizza box on the ground beside the tree.

"Don't get me wrong," Berry explained to the cat as she scrambled to shinny up the tree. "It's not that I don't like kittens. And it isn't that I mind climbing trees. It's just that I've about filled my good deed quota this week." She grasped at the lowest limb and hauled herself up in perfect tomboy fashion. "Do you know what I did this week, kitty? I advertised for a delivery boy, and then I hired three little old ladies instead. Now they're doing the baking, and I'm doing the delivering." Berry stopped to catch her breath. "I'm not a delivery sort of person. I get lost a lot, and I'm not too brave about knocking on strange doors. And if that isn't bad enough, I moved the old ladies into my apartment."

The kitten looked at her and blinked.

Berry sighed in exasperation. "Well, what could I do? They were living in the train station."

Berry wriggled next to the kitten and looked up toward the stars. It was nice in the tree. The wind whistled through the limbs and whipped her short hair around her face.

"People should sit in trees more often," she said to the cat. "It's peaceful and exciting, all at the same time. And you can see forever. Practically clear down to the little bridge at the lower end of Ellenburg Drive."

She watched in quiet fascination as headlights smoothly moved over the bridge and snaked uphill toward her. The soft rumble of an expensive car broke the silence.

"Just great," she breathed, suddenly aware of her predicament. "Large Pizza with the Works is coming home, and I'm sitting in his tree!"

A Great Gatsby–type car purred up the driveway. It was a large, cream-colored machine with a brown leather convertible top, spoked wheels, and running boards. The garage doors automatically opened, swallowed up the antique car, and closed with a neat click, plunging Berry and the cat back into quiet darkness.

Berry exhaled a low whistle. "Impressive," she remarked to the cat. "What was that? A

Stutz Bearcat? Or maybe a Stanley Steamer? Definitely something old and flashy, and perfectly restored. I'll say this for Quasi, he has style and money. I bet he's some eccentric gangster. Some drug runner who's watched too many old movies."

Berry imagined him as looking like Quasimodo in a panama hat. The white pizza box on the ground caught her attention. She should probably deliver it, she thought guiltily. Quasimodo was home now and might be hungry. After all, she did take pride in her job.

"Neither rain, nor sleet, nor snow shall keep me from delivering pizza," Berry explained to the kitten. Of course there was nothing in that zippy little slogan about weird people and spooky houses. Maybe what she'd do was leave the box on the porch, ring the bell, and run like heck. She tucked the kitten under her arm. "Don't worry, cat," she whispered. "If I got up this tree, I can get down this tree."

Berry slithered toward the trunk, looking for a branch within stepping range. A hall light sparkled at the other side of the house, and then a light flashed on directly in front of her. It was a bedroom. Quasi's bedroom. And she was sitting eye level to it, getting a crystal-clear picture of the most mouthwatering male she'd ever seen—more than six feet tall with broad shoulders and slim hips and wavy almost-black hair that curled over his ears and scraped his crisp white shirt collar. Definitely not Quasimodo.

He flung a book onto the bed and popped the top button of his shirt open. Then another button. Then another. Berry involuntarily inched closer to the window. After all, she rationalized, if he was a gangster she would need to be able to give the FBI a detailed description. She should watch closely and check for hidden weapons and identifying scars.

He pulled the shirt off and draped it over a chair. Berry closed her eyes for a split second, swallowed, and made a mental note that there was no hunchback on Quasi. Just lots of muscle in all the right places, and a flat stomach with a thin line of black hair, leading to his . . . Holy cow! He was unzipping his pants.

Berry panicked.

"I've got to get down," she whispered to the cat. "I've got to get out of here."

Berry desperately looked for a foothold, willing her eyes to behave themselves and not return to the window. This wasn't the sort of thing pizza delivery ladies were supposed to do. Peeping in men's bedroom windows was a definite no-no. It was rude and immoral and could get you into a whole bunch of trouble. In fact, Berry decided, there was something about this man that smacked of trouble. He had the ability to fascinate, to mesmerize, to incite riot in a woman's body . . . in *her* body. Berry's body hadn't rioted in a long time. Working fourteen hours a day making pizzas didn't leave much time or energy for romance. Lately she'd been convinced her hormones were in premature retirement, but there was something about this man that caught their attention. The way he moved with the fluid efficiency of an athlete, plus something else, something more elusive than perfectly toned muscle. There was a good-humored set to his mouth.

Berry's pulse quickened. With or without clothes, the man was a menace to mental health and glandular stability. And she was dying to take one more peek. Her eyes focused on Mr.

Large Pizza with the Works. He had stripped to a pair of navy bikini briefs. He stuck his thumbs into the elastic waistband, gave a downward tug, and . . .

"Holy cow!" Berry gasped, covering her face with her hands. Her heart jumped to her throat, she lost her balance and went over backward, tail over teakettle, frantically grasping for branches as she fell, her leg scraping against a lower limb as it cracked under her falling weight. Then *whump*! She landed flat on her back, knocking the air out of her lungs. Little black dots floated in front of her eyes, and the ocean was pounding in her ears.

A few seconds—or was it hours?—later, Berry blinked at the hunk of masculinity that bent over her. "Am I dead?"

"Not yet."

"I feel dead. I must be bleeding. My back is all warm and sticky."

The hunk squatted beside her and looked more closely. "I don't see any blood, just some pizza sauce oozing through this crumpled box. Lady, you've squished this poor pizza to smithereens." He extracted the pizza box. "Is this mine?"

Berry nodded. She was relieved to find that he was fully clothed in a pair of jeans and a navy hooded sweatshirt. She made an attempt to sit up and began a methodical check of any bones that might be broken.

"What happened?" he asked. "I heard something crashing around out here, and there you were, flat out on my pizza. Are you okay?"

He picked bits of bark from her tangled hair. He glanced at the profusion of broken branches scattered on the ground and his attention turned to the tree, his gaze traveling up the height of it, resting on the large limb just outside his bedroom window. Incredulity registered on his face.

"Lady, you must be kidding! You can't be that hard up to see a naked man."

"I'm not hard up at all," Berry said with a toss of her head. "I've seen lots of naked men."

He raised his eyebrows. "Lots?"

"Well, maybe not lots. A few. Actually, not too many." She threw her hands into the air in frustration. "Well, dammit, I've been busy. I don't have time to go around looking at naked men. I have a pizza business to run. I have old ladies to take care of. And anyway, you've got this all wrong. I was rescuing a kitten."

They both looked up at the tree. No kitten.

Berry pointed. "There was a kitten up there!"

"Uh-huh."

The hunk didn't believe her! Of all the nerve. Berry tipped her nose up and gave him her most withering look. Well, phooey on you, her most withering look said. I don't care what you think, anyway. She retrieved the crumpled pizza box and thrust it into his hands. "Here, this is yours. Seventeen ninety-five, please."

He looked down at the flattened box that was oozing pizza sauce. "Shouldn't I get a disaster discount?"

Berry had to admit, seventeen ninety-five was a little high for a smashed pizza. "Fine," she said, "it's on the house."

"Thanks. The strip show is on the house, too," he said, smiling. "Now we're even."

Berry looked at him. Two eyebrows, nice nose, suspicious brown eyes. And a mouth that looked like it might be laughing at her. His mouth wasn't too big, and wasn't too small, and it was slightly turned up at the corners. Truth was, it was probably the greatest mouth she'd ever seen.

"Are you going to kiss me?" he asked.

Berry snapped to attention. "Certainly not!"

Laugh lines crinkled around his eyes. "You were staring at my mouth."

"I thought it might be laughing at me."

He looked at her tangled blond curls, big blue eyes, and cute little nose. And he looked at her mouth. Full and soft. *Not* smiling. His gaze moved south over her red down vest, long-sleeved shirt, and faded jeans. She was slim. Maybe five-five. Hard to tell her age. Somewhere between sixteen and thirty-two, he guessed. He hoped she wasn't sixteen because he was having thoughts about her that would be inappropriate if she was sixteen.

"Jake Sawyer," he said, extending his hand. "How old are you?"

"I'm too close to thirty."

"I suppose you're the owner of that dilapidated Jeep."

"That Jeep is *not* dilapidated. That Jeep is almost in A-one condition."

As if on cue, there was a loud *spronnnng* at curbside, and the Jeep slowly began rolling backward, down Ellenburg Drive.

Berry gasped. "My Jeep!"

The Jeep picked up speed on a downhill curve, jumped the curb, merrily bounced over a grassy area, and headed for an opening between two large birch trees. Berry took off running and raced alongside, trying to get a grip on the door handle. Her fingers had just touched metal when Sawyer tackled her, and they both went down to the ground. She picked her head up in time to see the Jeep squeeze between the two trees and catapult itself off a twenty-foot cliff.

"Get off!" she said, twisting under Sawyer. "You must weigh two hundred pounds."

"One-eighty and it's all muscle."

Berry already knew the part about it being all magnificent muscle. Besides being permanently engraved in her brain, she could feel it being firmly pressed into her. His knee was cozily nudged against the inside of her leg, and his delicious mouth was hovering just inches above her own.

"You're staring at my mouth again," he said.

And he kissed her. Nothing serious. Just a single, testing-the-waters kiss.

"Jeez," Berry said.

"Is that good or bad?"

It was terrific, Berry thought. Not that she would admit it to Mr. Large Pizza.

"It was entirely inappropriate," she said, wriggling out from under him, getting to her feet. "And that was *my* Jeep. I needed it. I can't deliver pizzas without it. You had no business jumping on me like that."

"Are you crazy? You would have killed yourself."

"Well, fine. Now I'll slowly die of starvation because I'm deprived of earning a living."

Good grief, Berry thought, she sounded like an uptight, whining moron. It was so unfair. Why couldn't she have met this gorgeous guy under more favorable circumstances? Like maybe winning him in the lottery. She turned on her heel and strode off to the birch trees to inspect the damage.

She'd gotten the Jeep two years ago, the day after her divorce had been finalized, and it had never given her a moment's trouble. Of course, she had to give it a quart of oil every Friday, she thought. And it did look a little disreputable with all that rust and the coat hanger antenna, but those things were cosmetic.

They stood at the edge of the cliff and gazed down at the Jeep, belly-up and slightly squashed in the moonlight.

Berry sighed in morose resignation. "It's dead."

"Doesn't look good."

Berry was at a loss for words. After all, what on earth can you say when your entire future has just gone over a cliff? What can you say when faced with certain bankruptcy? And I'm not going to cry, she told herself, frowning. I absolutely am not going to cry.

He studied her face in the moonlight. "You're not going to cry, are you?"

"Absolutely not." A large tear oozed over her lower lashes and streaked down her cheek. "Damn."

She was pretty, he thought. And she was nice to kiss. But she was a little nutty. Not that he would hold that against her. He put an arm around her shoulders and wiped the tear away with his thumb.

"It's okay," Jake said. "The insurance will pay to replace your car."

Berry slumped and did another sigh.

"You don't have insurance," he guessed.

"Not that kind. Only if I run over somebody." She squared her shoulders and turned on her heel. "Well, good-bye."

Good-bye? He wasn't ready for good-bye. He wanted to look at the blond curls some more. He needed to know *why* she didn't have insurance. And what was her favorite ice cream flavor? And when was her birthday? And was she really okay after falling out of his tree? And in fact, he wouldn't mind knowing what she thought of him naked, but probably he shouldn't rush that one.

He walked beside her. "Where are you going?"

"Home."

"That must be miles from here."

Berry shrugged. "It's not so far."

May as well get used to walking, she thought, I'm going to be doing a lot of it. Anyway, she could use the exercise to get rid of the nervous stomach caused by Mr. Large Pizza with the Works and his navy briefs.

No way was she walking home, Jake thought. It was dark, and late. She could get mugged or snatched by a maniac serial rapist. And she smelled like pizza. She could get attacked by a pack of hungry dogs.

"If you'll wait a minute, I'll give you a ride," he said to her.

"Thanks, but that's not necessary. Besides, I'd get your fancy car all dirty."

"My fancy car has leather seats. They wash. Wait here."

Berry kept walking. "Really, it's not necessary."

He grabbed her firmly by the shoulders and plunked her into a sitting position on the edge of the curb. "Wait here!"

"You're awfully bossy."

"So I've been told."

That intrigued her. She watched him jog away and wondered who else thought he was bossy. A girlfriend, maybe? A wife? She was still wondering when the cream-colored car rolled to a stop in front of her. She removed her vest and carefully placed it on the floor, mozzarella side up.

"This is very nice of you," Berry said.

"Yup, that's me. I'm an all-around nice guy." He cut his eyes to her. "You haven't told me your name."

"Berry Knudsen."

"Berry? Like in holly berry or cranberry?"

"Lingonberry. My mother was inordinately proud of her Scandinavian heritage. So, who else thinks you're bossy? Your wife?"

Sawyer mumbled something unintelligible.

"Excuse me?"

"My kids," he said on a sigh.

His kids? He had kids. And a wife. And he'd just kissed her. She was going to go straight home and brush her teeth.

"How many kids do you have?" she asked.

"Twenty-one. This morning they all told me the same thing you did. They think I'm bossy."

"Twenty-one kids?"

"I teach first grade."

"So you're not married?'

"No."

Berry almost swooned with relief. He wasn't married. Not that it really mattered to her. She wasn't interested in men right now. She especially wasn't interested in this man. Still, it was good to know she hadn't kissed a philanderer. She hadn't spied on someone else's private property. She hadn't smashed a family pizza. And this tantalizing hunk of manliness, driving a megabucks car, taught first grade. Imagine that!

"You don't look like a first-grade teacher," she said.

Jake let out a low groan. "I know. I'm too big. I don't fit in any of the little chairs. My fingers aren't good at holding crayons or safety scissors. And I can't get the hang of barrettes at all." He slumped in his seat. "I wasn't cut out for first grade. This is the toughest thing I've ever done."

The image of Jake Sawyer playing mother hen to a group of seven-year-olds brought a smile to Berry's lips. If she'd had a first-grade teacher that looked like Jake Sawyer, she'd have done anything to stay after school. Her first-grade teacher had been five feet, two inches tall and weighed close to two hundred pounds. Mrs. Berman. Berry shivered at the memory.

"Earth to Berry."

"Sorry. I guess I drifted off."

"I was afraid you might have sustained a head injury when you fell out of the tree."

"No. The only thing damaged is my pride and your pizza." She squinted into the darkness. "Turn right at the next light. Then just go straight until you see the sign, PIZZA PLACE."

"This isn't exactly a ritzy part of town."

Berry shrugged. "It's an ethnic neighborhood. Italian bakery. Vietnamese laundry. Ethiopian restaurant. Everybody's struggling to make a start, like me."

Jake executed a smooth corner at the light and frowned at the dark street lined with grimy stores and intersected by narrow alleyways. "Why have you chosen to work in this pizza place?"

"Why did you choose to teach first grade?"

Jake smiled wryly. "If I tell you, will you tell me?"

"I hope your story's more interesting than mine."

"I invented Gunk."

"Gunk?"

"It creeps. It crawls. It comes in five scents and three flavors. It's edible. It's freezable. It's disgusting."

"I've seen it advertised on television."

"I invented it. I was working for Bartlow Labs, looking for an inexpensive organic glue, and I discovered Gunk."

"Are you a chemist?"

"I used to be. I quit the second I sold my Gunk rights. I hated the fluorescent lights and the nine-to-five routine. And it was boring. Glue is boring." He smiled proudly. "Now I'm an inventor."

"What about teaching first grade?"

"Guinea pigs. I have twenty-one kids to test my new ideas. Besides, I had a teaching degree and I needed the money. I squandered my Gunk money on this car and that monstrous Victorian house."

Berry wrinkled her nose. The man had forsaken a respectable profession to invent future Gunk, and thought of seven-year-olds as guinea pigs. Prince Charming had some frog in him.

"How did you ever get the school board to hire you?"

"Luckily, Mrs. Newfarmer had a nervous breakdown and suddenly abandoned her first-grade class. When I applied for a job as substitute teacher, they were desperate enough to consider me."

"Nervous breakdown? Must be some group of kids."

"The kids are terrific. Mrs. Newfarmer had marital problems."

Hmmm, she thought, I can relate to that. Marriage could easily give somebody a nervous breakdown. It could give you hives, and dishpan hands, and paranoia.

Berry knew firsthand. She had tried marriage. Four years of struggling to put her husband through medical school, and then she'd found him playing doctor with Mary Lou Marowski. Yes sir, she knew all about marriage.

"Well? What about you? Why are you working in this neighborhood?" he asked.

"I was married while still in college. We couldn't both afford to go to school full-time, so I quit and went to work. When my marriage fell apart after four years I didn't think I could manage a job that required much mental concentration or emotional energy. I wanted something to do with my hands. Something that was physically exhausting. And I wanted something that was close to the university so I could return to school part-time. Well, here it is. The Pizza Place. I worked as a pizza maker for a year, and when the owner retired seven months ago, I scraped together every cent I could find, mortgaged my soul, and bought the business."

Jake parked at the curb and considered the two-story yellow brick building. A gaudy red neon sign flashed out PIZZA PLACE in the ground-floor picture window. White ruffled curtains hung in the four second-story windows.

"You live upstairs?" he asked.

"Yup."

"Alone?"

"Not anymore. I adopted three old ladies this week."

Jake raised his eyebrows.

"It's a long story."

Berry eased herself out of the car, relieved to say good-bye to Jake Sawyer. The man was physically disturbing. He gave her hot flashes. She wasn't even sure if she liked him. He bought extravagant cars and eccentric houses. He thumbed his nose at security. The man was a risk taker with big dreams.

Berry had small dreams. She wanted a college education. She wanted a window that overlooked a meadow, or a creek, or a green lawn bordered by flower beds. She wanted a nice, boring husband who believed in monogamy, but she didn't want him now. First the college education, then the husband, then the lawn. That was The Plan. It certainly didn't include breaking out in a sweat over awesome Jake Sawyer. And the worst part about all this was that she'd acted so dopey! She'd fallen out of his tree onto a pizza. Yeesh.

Berry mumbled an embarrassed thank-you, carefully closed the door of Jake's expensive car, and beat a hasty retreat to her apartment. Her back ached, her arms were scratched, and her jeans had a large hole in the knee. Not one of her better days. She'd peeked in Jake Sawyer's bedroom window and ogled his body, and now she was being punished. How else could you explain the Jeep suicide? Berry trudged up the narrow stairs. At least the score should be even now. Her Jeep for thirty seconds of Jake Sawyer practically nude. It seemed like a fair price, but she didn't know how she was ever going to replace the stupid Jeep. She didn't have a dime in the bank, and she had nowhere to go for credit. What a rotten break. Just when she was making some progress. Last week she'd gotten two lunch contracts at local businesses. How was she going to deliver pizzas without the Jeep?

"Damn," she said, trudging up the narrow stairs. "Double damn."

Mrs. Dugan stood ramrod-straight with righteous indignation at the head of the stairs. "Hmmm, fine talk for a young lady. I may as well tell you right now, I don't tolerate cussing."

A second gray-haired lady appeared in the doorway. "For goodness' sakes, Sarah, all she said was *damn. Damn* doesn't hardly count as a cussword. Young people say things like that nowadays."

A third voice chimed in. "You're right, Mildred, what should she say? Oh, fudge? Darn?

It's not the same, not the same at all. Sometimes you need to let loose with a good cuss. In fact, I feel like cussing right now." The plump old lady uttered an expletive that made double damn sound like polite conversation and raised everyone's eyebrows, including Berry's.

"Mrs. Fitz!"

Mrs. Fitz slapped her leg and laughed out loud. "That was a beauty, wasn't it? See, I feel much better now."

Berry wearily walked across the room and sank into the Boston rocker.

"Good heavens," Mrs. Fitz exclaimed. "What happened to you? You're a mess."

"I fell out of a tree onto the large pizza with the works. And then the Jeep drove itself over a cliff."

Mrs. Dugan set a bowl of soapy water at Berry's feet and began gently dabbing at her scratched cheek. "You aren't hurt serious, are you? You have anything worse than these scratches and scrapes?"

"Nope, I'm okay."

Berry smiled. It had been a long time since she'd had this sort of motherly attention. Her own mother was miles away in McMinneville, Oregon, and Allen, her ex-husband, had never given her much attention. She was still amazed at how marriage could be such a lonely way of life. Four years of living with a man who never remembered her birthday or noticed a wayward tear. She'd been so impressed with his cool intelligence and professional aspirations that she'd jumped into marriage without considering his emotional limitations. Thank goodness all that was behind her. She was older and wiser and pleased with her hard-won independence.

"Hello," Jake Sawyer called from the top of the stairs.

"Goodness," Mrs. Fitz exclaimed, "who's the hunk?"

"I'm Berry's friend."

Mrs. Dugan gaped at him in dumbfounded silence, her hand frozen in midair.

Jake noticed the water and blood dripping from Berry's arm and gently removed the wet cloth from Mrs. Dugan's fingers. He soaked the cloth and applied it to Berry's scratches.

Having Mrs. Dugan swab away the dirt and blood was one thing. Having Jake Sawyer minister to her wounds was another. It was disturbingly tender and caring and absolutely unwanted. Berry clenched her teeth, narrowed her eyes, and hoped she looked menacing.

"What are you doing here?" she asked Sawyer.

"Damned if I know," he said. "I was sitting down there at the curb and couldn't get myself to drive off. I kept getting this mental picture of you standing out on the highway, thumbing a ride with a pizza box stuck under your arm."

"So?"

"So I didn't like it." His dark eyes searched hers. "You're really in a bind, aren't you?"

"I'll figure something out."

Jake's mouth quirked into an embarrassed grin. "I have a confession to make. That was my neighbor's cat in the tree. She gets up there all the time."

Berry's eyes opened wide. "You acted like I was a Peeping Tom."

"Well? Were you peeping?"

"Only a little!"

She felt her blood pressure rise. It wasn't her fault. She had been in that tree doing a good deed, and he'd practically flaunted himself at her. She sprang out of the chair and stood with her fists on her hips.

"What was I supposed to do? You got undressed right in front of the window. Don't you believe in shades? What are you, some kind of exhibitionist?"

"I just moved in. I haven't had time to put shades up. Anyway, there aren't any neighbors for miles."

Berry turned on her heel and glared at the three ladies who were "tsking" behind her. She frowned and gave a look that said, One word out of any of you and it's back to the train station.

Jake held his hands up. "Wait. I didn't come up here to discuss your voyeuristic tendencies."

"Voyeuristic tendencies! Of all the . . . You are the most . . . I am not!"

Berry closed her eyes and took several deep breaths. She opened her eyes and made a flamboyant gesture with her arm, pointing to the door.

"Out!"

Jake took a seat in the vacant rocking chair

and accepted a cup of cocoa from Mrs. Fitz. "Boy, she sure can get riled," he said.

"Yeah, ain't she a pip?"

That was the perfect description, Jake thought. Berry Knudsen was a pip. He'd dated lots of women and none of them had been exactly right, and now he realized none of them had been a *pip*.

Berry spun around and flapped her arms at Mrs. Fitz. "Mrs. Fitz, anyone can see this man is leaving. We don't serve cocoa to men who are leaving."

"Nonsense. He's all settled in here." Mrs. Fitz pressed her lips together in satisfaction. "Don't he look nice and comfy."

Mildred Gaspich brought him a plate of chocolate chip cookies. "We just baked these fresh tonight." She turned to Mrs. Fitz. "Goodness, it's nice to have a man in the house."

"Makes me want to put on some fresh lipstick." Mrs. Fitz laughed. "Too bad I haven't got any."

Miss Gaspich put her arm around plump little Lena Fitz. "That's okay. Pretty soon you'll have money to buy some lipstick."

"Berry's hired us," Mrs. Fitz explained to Jake.

"We were just about scraping by on our social security checks, living in the Southside Hotel for Ladies, and then they decided to renovate the building and turn it into fancy condominiums. We couldn't afford anyplace else. We looked real hard, but there just wasn't a room cheap enough. Finally, they evicted us. We were temporarily holed up in the train station when we saw Berry's ad in the paper."

Mrs. Fitz grinned. She was five feet tall with short steel-gray hair that had been permed into two inches of frizz. She was apple-cheeked, with an ample chest and dimples in her elbows and stout knees.

"We know we're a bunch of old ladies," Mrs. Fitz said, "but we figured the three of us together might be able to hold down a job. Sort of a package deal."

Miss Gaspich pulled a kitchen chair close to the rocker. "We walked all over town for days trying to get a job and then Berry hired us. We'd just about given up."

"This business with the Jeep isn't gonna change things, is it?" Mrs. Fitz worried. "How bad is the Jeep?"

"All the king's horses and all the king's men can't put the Jeep back together again," Berry told her.

Jake downed the last of the cocoa and stood to leave. "It's okay, Mrs. Fitz. Berry's going to use my car until she can replace the Jeep."

Berry looked at him wide-eyed. "I can't deliver pizzas in your car."

Jake somberly chewed a cookie. "It was my cat that started this fiasco. I feel responsible."

He leaned close to Berry and whispered in an aside, "Besides, I liked kissing you."

Berry ignored the heat that burned in her cheeks. "I can't deliver pizzas in a megabucks car!"

Mrs. Fitz whistled behind her. "You mean he looks like this, and he's rich, too?"

"I invented Gunk."

Mrs. Fitz's eyes popped wide open. "That disgusting slimy stuff you can eat? I love that stuff."

Jake turned to Berry. "My school is just three blocks from here. I'll drop the car off on my way to work tomorrow morning."

Chapter 2

Berry looked at the stacks of pizza boxes and wondered how she was ever going to get them all into Jake Sawyer's two-seater. Eighteen large pizzas and seven small, all due at Windmere Technicals by twelve-thirty. She groaned. If it hadn't been for these lunch contracts she would never have accepted Jake's offer. The car was too expensive, too powerful, too exotic. What if she scratched it? The car was perfect, for crying out loud. How could anything that old look so new? We aren't talking about a two-hundred-dollar Jeep here. We're talking about an outrageously extravagant toy in mint condition.

And what about Jake Sawyer? Another extravagant toy, Berry thought. Too powerful, too expensive, too exotic . . . and in mint condition. She'd spent half the night reviewing his kiss and knew it was in her best interest to not have a repeat performance. Berry had interrupted her education once for a man, and she wasn't about to make the same mistake again. She would borrow Jake's car only until she could find a better solution to her problem, and she would steer clear of its owner.

She speared the car keys with her pinky finger and pushed through the front door, balancing six large pizza boxes in her outstretched arms. She squinted into the light drizzle, wondering where Jake had parked. He'd said the car was directly in front of the Pizza Place. Berry held the door open with her foot.

"Mrs. Fitz," she called over her shoulder. "You took the keys from Jake this morning. Where'd he park the car?"

Mrs. Fitz wiped her hands on her big white apron and shook her head. "Goodness' sakes, child, the car's right in front of you. It's right here in front of the store." Mrs. Fitz walked to the front of the store, and her eyes opened extra wide. "Where's the car?"

"Maybe Jake moved it. Maybe he changed his mind."

"I don't think so. We've got his keys."

Berry felt her heart stutter. Jake's expensive car was missing.

"There's probably a simple explanation," she said.

"Yup," Mrs. Fitz said. "The explanation is simple all right. Someone stole Jake's car."

Berry staggered back into the store and deposited the pizza boxes on the counter. The car was stolen! She'd had possession of it exactly three and a half hours, and it now had gotten itself stolen. How was that possible? Why hadn't they seen it happening?

"Jake's not gonna be happy about this," Mrs. Fitz said, shaking her head.

"One minute it was there, and then the next minute . . . poof!" Berry said.

"It was like aliens took it," Mrs. Fitz said. "Like they just beamed it up. Right out from under our noses." Mrs. Fitz dialed a number. "I'm calling a taxi so I can deliver the pizzas. You stay here and call the police. Maybe they'll get the car back before Jake gets out of school."

Berry's face brightened. That was a hopeful

thought. It wasn't exactly run-of-the-mill. The police would probably have an easy time finding it.

Four hours later, Mrs. Fitz placed a plate of cookies and a glass of milk in front of Jake. "It's not so bad. Nobody's been hurt. You just lost your car for a while."

Jake stared glassy-eyed at the cookies, mumbling things Berry couldn't quite catch. Things that might sound like . . . I knew I was doomed the minute I saw her.

Mrs. Dugan patted his hand. "We filed a police report. The officers said they'd be sure to find an unusual car like that."

"It's unique. I had it specially restored. There's not another one like it in the whole world."

Be sympathetic, Berry thought. Remember how devastated you were when your car jumped off that cliff?

Yes, she answered herself, but I needed that car to exist. *This* car was a toy. And *this* car was insured.

Berry, Berry, Berry, she chanted. Men love their toys. And everyone knows there's this whole complicated connection between men and their cars and their cock-a-doodle. Although from what she'd seen, Jake's cock-a-doodle really didn't need automotive fortification. Still, it was hard to be sympathetic when there was that business with him mumbling about being doomed. She suspected he was mumbling about her . . . as if she was a disaster or something.

She pounded pizza dough on the large wooden counter behind Jake. I am *not* a disaster, she thought. Okay, so I fell out of a tree. Big deal. It could happen to anyone. And then my Jeep committed suicide. I don't really see where that was my fault. Finally, did I ask him to loan me his car? No! Did I tell him to park it on this street? No! And I didn't ask him to kiss me, either!

Mrs. Fitz peered across the counter at Berry. "Good heavens, child, you're just about beating that poor dough to death."

Berry blew out a sigh. For a full year after her divorce she'd taken her frustrations out on pizza dough. If it hadn't been for pizza dough she might have turned into a homicidal maniac. Then little by little her life had fallen into place, her sunny disposition had returned, peace and purpose had replaced the disorder of disillusionment.

Berry poked at the massacred lump. She'd known Jake Sawyer for less than twenty-four hours and here she was smashing innocent pizza dough again. The man was a threat to her sanity. He gave her an upset stomach. He made her act like a boob, blushing and stammering and falling out of trees.

You don't need this, Berry thought, taking a vicious swipe at the dough with her wooden rolling pin. Someday she would be ready for another relationship—but not now. First, she had to get the Pizza Place on its feet. Second, she'd get her bachelor's degree. Third . . .

Third was interrupted by the phone ringing. Mrs. Fitz answered and smiled. "It's the police. They've found the car!"

Jake stared at the address Mrs. Fitz had written. "The corner of Grande and Seventeenth Street."

Berry pulled her quilted vest over a gray hooded sweatshirt. "I know where that is. It's less than half a mile from here. We can walk."

Jake stood in the doorway, zipped his parka, and took a grim assessment. A cold mist drizzled down the grimy brick facades of nearby stores, and intermittent gusts of wind buffeted plate-glass windows. Sodden newspapers and assorted litter slapped against doorways and clogged gutters. This part of town wasn't attractive, and it obviously wasn't safe. And it was *not* the ideal neighborhood for a defenseless, pretty little blond and three little old ladies, Jake thought.

Berry knew what Jake was seeing. He was seeing bars at first-floor windows installed to prevent burglaries. He was seeing the empty beer cans and wine bottles that hadn't made it into trash cans. He was imagining thugs lurking in the alleys, and poverty hiding behind closed doors.

"It's not all that bad," Berry said to Jake. "You see that cheery yellow light in the window above Giovanni's Grocery? That's Mrs. Giovanni making supper. In the summer she hangs window boxes from her kitchen window and fills them with red geraniums. The apartment building next to me houses four generations of Lings. Last year Charlie Ling won first prize at his school science fair."

"So you really like this neighborhood?"

Berry shrugged. "It's okay. I'd rather look out my window and see a meadow or a mountain, but instead I have Mrs. Giovanni's bold red geraniums. I try to make the best of it."

Jake smiled down at her. Damned if she wasn't getting to him. He added *loyal* and *positive* to his earlier assessments of *kind to old ladies*, *resilient*, and *slightly daffy*.

Nice smile, Berry thought, but she was pretty sure she didn't want to know what was going on inside his head. He looked like the wolf that wanted to eat Red Riding Hood's grandma.

"This way," Berry said, heading for Grande.

Jake snagged her arm. "Hold it, Goldilocks, where's your umbrella?"

"I don't own an umbrella."

"Then at least put your hood up."

"I hate wearing hoods."

"Mrs. Dugan would take her wooden spoon to you if she caught you out in the rain like this without a hat."

"Back off!" Berry said.

Jake Sawyer mentally checked off the boxes labeled *temper* and *stubborn*. And then he decided it was all adorable on her, so he kissed her.

"Good grief," Berry said.

Jake rocked back on his heels and smiled. He was infatuated.

"I have to admit, it's a little unnerving knowing you've seen me naked," he said to Berry. Actually, *unnerving* wasn't precisely correct, Jake thought. A better word might be *erotic*.

"I didn't see you naked. I fell out of the tree before you got to the really good stuff."

Jake was glad she thought he had good stuff, but he was sort of disappointed she hadn't seen it. He'd had a really good fantasy going for a while there.

He pulled her hood over her head and tied the drawstring securely into a bow in his best first-grade-teacher fashion. Without saying another word he took her hand and pulled her along beside him.

As they approached Grande Street Berry felt his grip tighten. Big, strong Jake Sawyer was nervous. He really did like his flashy car. Berry didn't know much about cars, but she knew about losing things you love. She knew about the pain and anxiety such a loss produced. Berry felt an overwhelming urge to rush out and buy Jake Sawyer a pint of his favorite ice cream. Instead she squeezed his hand and sent him her most comforting smile.

He glanced down at her. "I'm kind of nervous."

"I guessed."

"Probably it's okay."

"Probably," Berry said, not entirely believing it. With the way her luck had been running, the car would be picked cleaner than a turkey carcass the day after Thanksgiving.

They turned the corner and found several officers standing hands on hips by a black-and-white squad car, inspecting an article at curbside. It took several seconds before Jake and Berry recognized the object of their curiosity. At first glance it seemed to be a piece of scrap metal resting on four cinder blocks.

Jake expelled a well-chosen expletive that caused the officers to turn in his direction.

"Is that my car?" Jake asked.

"If you're Jake Sawyer, that's your car. What's left of it," one of the cops said.

Jake stretched his hands out in despair. "What the . . . oh . . . man! Look at this. How could this happen so fast?"

"Modern technology," one of the cops said.

Jake kicked at the cinder block and swore some more.

Berry trotted beside him as he paced back and forth the length of the car carcass. "It's not so bad. The insurance will buy you a new one. You do have insurance, don't you?"

"Of course I have insurance. Who cares about insurance? This car was irreplaceable."

"Nonsense. There must be parts somewhere. Just put it back together."

"Put it back together? Berry, this isn't a fruitcake we're talking about. This was an exquisitely tuned, handcrafted piece of machinery. This was a part of history." Jake stopped pacing and plunged his hands into his pockets. "Anyway, this was my Gunk car. It was special," he added quietly.

Berry was beginning to understand why he loved the flashy car so much. He'd given himself a present. It wasn't just a car, it represented a new life. No more fluorescent lights. No more boring glue. She thought maybe squandering all his money on a house and a car had been an act of confidence for Jake Sawyer. It was a way of saying, It's okay to spend all the Gunk money, because I'm going to be a success at my new career. I'm going to make a lot more money. And now he'd lost his Gunk car, and maybe he was a little afraid he'd never be able to replace it.

Jake turned to the officer. "Do you know who did this?"

"We'll ask around. Sometimes we get lucky and come up with a name."

Jake stared morosely at his car. "This is damn depressing."

Berry linked her arm through his and narrowed her eyes in mock annoyance. "This will never do, Sawyer," she said. "You're an inventor. You're supposed to be happy."

"Yeah, but this sad hunk of scrap metal was my toy."

"Don't you have any other toys?"

He shook his head. "I'm really a very dull person. Work, work, work."

"That was back in your glue days. Now you're an inventor. Now it's play, play, play."

He studied her for a moment. She was trying to cheer him up. And she was doing a halfway okay job of it.

"Are you sure you didn't see me naked?" he asked her.

Berry opened one eye and grimaced. Six o'clock in the morning and Mrs. Fitz was making tea.

"Mrs. Fitz, don't you ever sleep?" Berry asked.

"Old people don't need so much sleep. Anyway, it isn't any fun sleeping with those two. They snore." Mrs. Fitz added a dollop of honey to her tea. "Now, if I had a man in my bed, well, that'd be something different."

Berry straightened her flannel nightie and swung her legs over the side of the couch. The large front room of her apartment served as living room, dining room, and efficiency kitchen. The other smaller room, her bedroom, had been turned into a dormitory for the ladies. She liked the ladies and enjoyed their company, but she dearly missed the comfort of her nice, big bed. She rubbed a sore spot on her back and slid her feet into a pair of slippers that looked like raccoons.

"Maybe you should remarry," Berry said. "Have you ever thought about finding a husband?"

"I've been looking around, but I haven't seen anything I like yet. Now if I was younger I'd go for that Jake Sawyer."

Berry filled the coffeemaker with water, added a couple scoops of coffee, and punched the go button. She had an economics quiz later that morning that she'd totally forgotten about. Twenty-four hours of Jake Sawyer and already she was neglecting her studies. She opened the refrigerator and rattled a bunch of jars around.

"What are you looking for?" Mrs. Fitz asked.

"My coffee mug."

"Lordy, child, you aren't going to find it in there."

"Oh, yeah."

Damn, she thought, this is what a sleepless night does to you. How could anyone get to sleep with visions of Jake Sawyer dancing in her head? Jake Sawyer in his one-of-a-kind car. Jake Sawyer in her kitchen. Jake Sawyer in his underwear. And she could swear he seemed disappointed that she hadn't seen him naked.

The man was downright disturbing. She found her coffee mug and filled it with prune juice.

Mrs. Fitz raised her eyebrows. "I hope you're planning on staying close to home today. That's a lot of prune juice."

Berry peered into her mug and wrinkled her nose. "Ugh. What is this?"

Mrs. Fitz rolled her eyes, dumped the juice down the drain, and rinsed out Berry's mug. She filled the mug with coffee and handed it to Berry. "When you fell out of that tree, did you land on your head?"

"No. I landed on my pizza."

Mrs. Fitz looked at her shrewdly. "You're kind of stuck on that Sawyer guy."

"More like he's stuck in my head. Isn't that the pits?"

Mrs. Fitz looked disgusted. "Good heavens you're a ninny."

Mrs. Dugan padded into the kitchen area. "Who's a ninny?"

"Lingonberry here. She thinks love's a waste of time."

"Humph. Sometimes it is. Remember William Criswald? The old coot. I fancied that man for seven years and just when I was about to reel him in, he died. The nerve. You can't count on men over seventy-five. You never know how long they're gonna last."

"Well, she isn't in love with an old goat like Criswald. She's in love with Jake Sawyer."

Berry slammed her coffee mug down on the counter, slopping hot coffee over her hand. "Ow! Dammit. I'm not in love with Jake Sawyer."

Mrs. Dugan and Mrs. Fitz exchanged glances and smiled slyly.

"I find him attractive, and I like him . . . usually," Berry said.

"She's in love with him, all right," Mrs. Fitz whispered to Mrs. Dugan.

Berry took a cautious sip of coffee and gathered her books together. "I can't be in love with someone I've only known for twenty-four hours."

"What about love at first sight?"

"It's a load of baloney. And besides, I refuse to be in love. I have other priorities, like taking an economics test that I'm totally unprepared for." She glanced at her watch and winced. She had no car, and she was late. "I have to run. I want to go to the library and try to get some studying in before my exam. Send the lunch contracts out by taxi again. I'll be back at three-thirty. Can you guys handle things?"

"Piece of cake."

Berry bolted down the stairs, only to be called back by Mrs. Fitz.

"Lingonberry," Mrs. Fitz shouted, "you're gonna look awful silly going to class in them raccoon slippers and your nightgown."

Berry crossed her fingers as she bounded down the stairs ten minutes later. Please God, no more disasters. She closed the door behind her and took a deep breath of cold crisp air. The rain had stopped during the night, and the neighborhood looked freshly washed and waiting for spring. Berry's mood was starting to improve with the promise of the new day.

She walked quickly, and two blocks later she found herself approaching the Willard Street Elementary School. Jake's school. She smiled at the old two-story, redbrick building. It brought back memories of her own school days in McMinneville, when each morning she would set off along quiet, tree-lined streets with her little sister, Katie.

It was a childhood of few surprises. Tuna fish or peanut butter and jelly in her lunch box. Hot oatmeal in the morning, homemade butterscotch pudding in the afternoon, and piano lessons every Thursday. The Knudsen household was middle-of-the-road and casually practical. Berry and Katie had worn sneakers and jeans and hand-embroidered shirts and hand-knit sweaters to school. They had a dress for church and they wore the dress with sturdy buckle shoes. No sneakers on Sunday.

Berry realized she'd been trying to reconstruct the stability of her childhood, with little success. Her mother had been a master of order and routine. Each mitten had its proper place, dinner was served promptly at five-thirty, the bathroom was always miraculously stocked with freshly laundered towels. It hadn't been a household of strict routine and unbending discipline. It had been a household of dull predictability and comfortable emotions.

My life is chaos, Berry groaned to herself. The harder I try, the worse it gets. I wash the towels, but I never get around to folding them. I lose mittens before I can find a proper place for them, and dinner consists of staring into the refrigerator at six-thirty and wondering what the devil I can eat in a hurry. Now I have three old ladies living with me and my refrigerator is filled with prune juice and blood pressure medicine. Berry shook her finger at the Willard School. And if that isn't bad enough I've got Jake Sawyer complicating things. Now not only are all my efforts at organization a total loss, but that rotten Jake Sawyer is destroying whatever emotional comfort I've managed to reinstate into my life.

"Why? Why me?" Berry pleaded out loud.

She quickly glanced around to make sure no one had noticed her talking to a school, glanced at her watch, and hurriedly moved on. She couldn't blame Jake and the school too much. Part of her problem was that days were too short. Twenty-four hours is simply not enough, she thought. If I had twenty-six I might have a chance to make butterscotch pudding once in a while.

Chapter 3

Berry saw the strange little puff of black smoke two and a half blocks away, but her mind was on other things—like her recent economics test and Jake Sawyer's smile. It wasn't until she turned the corner and saw the fire trucks that her mind contemplated disaster. Her heart skipped a beat and then felt as if it had stopped altogether. The trucks were in front of the Pizza Place. Fire hoses snaked across the sidewalk. Soot blackened the second-floor windows.

Berry clapped her hand to her mouth. "Oh, Lord, no!"

Mrs. Dugan, Mrs. Fitz, and Miss Gaspich were supposed to be safely housed in that building. At this time of the afternoon they would be taking naps and making tea. Please, please, please, Berry pleaded, let them be okay. Please don't let them be behind those four fire-blackened windows.

Berry stumbled into the street and broke into a run. Her chest was tight with fear, her vision blurred by the pounding of her heart. How could you grow to love three little old ladies so quickly? she wondered. She'd known them less than a week, but they'd become a precious part of her life.

She slowed to a jog when she caught sight of the women standing behind a fire truck. They were safe!

And then *wonk*! Instant black.

Minutes later Berry struggled through the murk of semiconsciousness. She opened her eyes and smiled. "Thanks for the pudding, Mom."

Jake tightened his grip on her. "What?"

"The pudding. It was great."

"Honey, I'm not your mom. Look at me."

Berry blinked and concentrated, shaking the last of the cobwebs away. Did she just call Jake Sawyer Mom? He felt like Mom. Strong and reassuring, pressing kisses against her temple, into her hair. She could get used to this. This could be habit-forming. Jake Sawyer was going to make some woman a wonderful mother . . . except he looked awful. Grime streaked his face, emphasizing the grim set to his mouth and the cold terror in his red-rimmed eyes. Berry touched her fingertip to a sweat-soaked ringlet that had fallen across his forehead. "You look terrible."

Jake broke into a grin, his teeth seeming extraordinarily white in the soot-darkened face. "I'm okay. Are you okay?"

"Of course."

"You got smacked in the head with a fire extinguisher that fell off the truck. It knocked you out."

"That's what happens to you when you don't make time for breakfast. You get wimpy. My mother warned me this would happen."

The stricken look left Jake's face and was replaced with an only moderately successful attempt at anger. "Don't ever skip breakfast again. It's enough to scare the daylights out of someone."

How great is this, Berry thought. No one was hurt, and Jake Sawyer was worried about me. Okay, so my apartment is trashed, and that's a bummer, but I've got a man hovering over me who seems to genuinely care if I live or die.

Jake looked at her carefully. "You sure you're okay? Your apartment just burned to a crisp, and you're grinning from ear to ear."

"I know. I can't help it." Berry pushed her mouth together with her fingers, trying to wipe away the smile. "I'll try to look more serious."

Mrs. Fitz dabbed at her nose with a tissue. "Lingonberry, I'm so sorry. It was all my fault. I got a nice big tip for delivering those pizzas, and I spent it on some newfangled electric curlers, and the dang things burned the apartment up."

Berry looked to Jake. "Is that true? Is that how the fire started?"

Jake nodded. "Mrs. Fitz plugged the curlers in to heat up, and then she set the case on the couch. Somehow, the curlers overheated and started to spark. The couch caught fire, then the curtain went up."

"How bad is it?"

"Could be worse. The fire was confined

to the couch area. Mostly what you've got is smoke damage. The downstairs wasn't affected at all."

"Can I go in?"

"Yeah. I just went through with the fire marshal. They're packing up to leave. You'll have to go down to the fire station later to fill out some forms."

Berry nodded and led the little parade of three ladies and Jake Sawyer up the stairs to her apartment. She walked into the middle of the living room, her feet squishing across the wet carpet, and blinked into the darkness. Everything was charcoal-gray. The walls, the ceilings, the rugs, the windows. The couch looked like it had been burned to cinders by the fire, stomped into oblivion by overzealous firefighters, and drowned.

"Yikes," Berry said.

"It makes a body want to cry to see it like this," Mrs. Fitz said. "It was so cozy."

"It'll never be the same," Mrs. Dugan said. "Everything in here smells like smoke. All our clothes, all the linens, all the tea bags."

Berry agreed. "It is pretty smoky. Tomorrow

morning we'll open the windows and try to air it out."

"Maybe we should go back to the train station for a while," Mildred said. "You could come with us, Lingonberry."

Jake gave a long-suffering, earth-rocking sigh. "Nobody's going to the train station. I have an empty house with plenty of space. You can all stay with me for a few days while we get the apartment cleaned."

Berry looked at him sidewise. "Are you sure you want to do this?"

He wanted Berry in his house, big time. Mrs. Fitz, Mrs. Dugan, and Miss Gaspich, no. They were nice ladies, but he had no desire to live with them. Problem was, he had even less desire to see them living at the train station.

"I'm sure," Jake said.

"A house!" Mrs. Fitz elbowed Mrs. Dugan. "Hear that? We're gonna live in a house."

Miss Gaspich carefully squished across the room. "I'll get my toothbrush and my nightie." She stopped at the bathroom door and gasped. She plucked a dingy gray object off the sink and held it up for inspection. "Is this my toothbrush?" Tears filled her round eyes and made streaks down her sooty, wrinkled cheeks. "That's the last straw. Even my toothbrush."

Jake gathered the ladies in his arms and ushered them down the stairs. "We can get new toothbrushes and clothes. Let's just get out of here for now. Everything will look better in the morning." He locked the apartment door, put the CLOSED sign in the window of the Pizza Place, and locked the front door. "I got a rental car today. It's just down the block."

Berry looked at Jake when they reached the car. It was a tan SUV.

"You don't seem like the SUV type," Berry said.

Jake helped Mrs. Dugan climb into the backseat. "I don't know what type I am. One minute I'm a carefree bachelor, riding high on Gunk, and then all of a sudden I've got a houseful of women. And none of them are any good for bachelor-type pursuits."

Berry rammed her hands onto her hips. "What's that supposed to mean? What do I look like, chopped liver?"

Jake tugged at a yellow curl. "I'm afraid,

Lingonberry, that you are very much like your name: delicious but virtually unobtainable. You would not be the first choice of a carefree bachelor. You are definitely *wife* material."

Berry thought about it for a moment and decided he was right. She wasn't much of a party girl. Even if she didn't have The Plan, she'd still be more apple pie than martini.

Jake cranked the SUV engine over, pulled away from the curb, and headed north.

"Hey, look at this," Mrs. Fitz exclaimed, ten minutes later. "We're out in the country. Isn't this something?"

"This isn't the country," Mrs. Dugan said. "This is the suburbs. You can tell the difference because the suburbs haven't got cows. There are cows in the country."

Berry tried to relax as the scenery on Ellenburg Drive flew by. Cows or not, in her book this was country. There were pretty houses, tucked back off the road with lots of space between them. The road narrowed to cross a good-sized creek and then began to snake uphill to Jake Sawyer's house. Berry felt as if she was going on vacation. She hadn't been on a vacation in six years, but going on vacation was like riding a bike—you never forgot the feeling.

There was a sense of expectation in the car. The air over the backseat fairly crackled with it as the ladies leaned forward in hushed anticipation, and in the front seat Berry couldn't have been more excited if she was spending a week at St. Moritz. She hugged herself and grinned. There would be lots of peace and quiet, and crickets chirping, and trees whooshing in the wind, and Jake Sawyer in his underwear. The image of Jake Sawyer in his sexy blue briefs was stuck in her brain like the refrain of a song that refused to be forgotten. Jake Sawyer in his underwear. How do you forget something like that?

Berry bit her lip, silently groaned, and rolled her window down a crack. It was getting warm in the car. This would never do. She had to put all this into proper perspective. This was not a vacation. And this was certainly not going to include Jake Sawyer in his you-know-what.

Mrs. Fitz poked her in the shoulder. "Are we almost there?"

"Yes," Berry said, "and this is not a vacation."

Mrs. Fitz shook her head. "What a ninny. Of course it's a vacation."

The house looked smaller and much less menacing by daylight. In fact, Berry decided it was downright cheerful. The house was bordered by dormant flower beds and a broad lawn. Several oak trees pressed their limbs toward the yellow siding. The lawn was surrounded by a buffer of woods. The white gingerbread trim sparkled in the sunshine. The front door was carved oak and topped with a stained glass window.

Mrs. Fitz gave a long, low whistle. "This is a pip of a house."

Berry stood in the foyer and admired the freshly waxed hardwood flooring, the hand-carved cherry banister that spiraled up the stairs, the ornate doorjambs. The entire downstairs had been painted a creamy white, giving the house a light, airy feeling. It contained few pieces of furniture. A large, overstuffed, buff-colored couch and matching club chair had been placed at the perimeters of an Oriental area rug in the living room. A pottery table lamp sat on the floor next to the chair. The foyer opened into a breakfast area at the rear of the house. A large round wood table nestled into the curve of a long bay window. It was a great house, Berry admitted. Worth every cent of Jake's Gunk money. And it deserved to have a terrific car sitting in its garage. She felt a true pang of remorse for the loss of the Gunk car. The car and the house belonged together.

"This is gonna be fun," Mrs. Fitz said. "I always wanted to live in a house like this. Boy, this feels like home. I could stay here forever. Come on, ladies, let's go upstairs and explore."

Berry caught the look of horror that passed through Jake's eyes and had to clap her hand over her mouth to keep from laughing.

Jake grabbed her by the nape of her neck. "I saw that smile. You've got a mean streak in you, Lingonberry Knudsen." His thumb massaged small circles on her neck just below her ear, and his muscled thigh grazed against her denim-clad leg. He put his mouth to her ear and spoke in a husky whisper. "She wouldn't really stay here forever, would she?"

"Mmmmm," Berry purred. "Mmmmaybe."

"And what about you?" Jake asked. "Will you stay forever?"

"I have a plan," Berry whispered.

Except The Plan was hazy when she was pressed against Jake like this and his thumb was doing those magical circles on her neck. The Plan seemed more like an *idea* she'd once had. The plan she had at the moment involved nibbling on Jake Sawyer's neck. Lord, he smelled good. Masculine—like musk cologne and campfire.

Her eyes opened wide. Crap. Hold the phone. Sawyer didn't smell like campfire. He smelled like her charcoal-roasted couch!

Jake stopped the massage and grinned at her. "Changed your mind?"

Berry blinked at him. "What do you mean?"

"For a minute there, you looked like you were contemplating nibbling on my neck."

"Jeez."

He stepped closer, backing Berry up against the foyer wall. "Just to get the record straight, I think I should tell you that it's okay for you to nibble on my neck any time you want. It isn't as if we're strangers, you know. After all, you've seen me in my underwear."

Berry stared at him in stoic resignation. They

were back to his underwear. This was never going to work. He had an evil sense of humor, he read minds, and he gave her a hormone attack just by lowering his voice an octave. "I think I should go home," Berry said, inwardly wincing when her voice cracked on the word *home*.

Jake shook his head. "Tsk, tsk, tsk. Where's your sense of adventure? Don't you want to be bold, like a red geranium?" His voice was teasing, but his eyes were serious, and the sexual tension stretched taut between them.

Berry gnawed on her lower lip. "Geraniums aren't in bloom yet. And neither am I," she added. "We're out of season."

Jake moved two inches closer, and Berry felt the panic rise in her throat as the tips of her breasts crushed against the wall of his chest. Oh, Lordy, she thought, he's going to kiss me again. He's going to plant those incredible lips of his on mine and melt the soles of my sneakers. She didn't know whether to close her eyes and pray it didn't happen, or leave her eyes open so she wouldn't miss a single thing. Jake lowered his mouth to hers before she had a chance to make a decision, and gave her a short, gentle kiss.

"Are you blooming, yet?" he whispered against her lips.

"No," she said. "I'm not even *nearly* blooming. I'm not going to bloom until I'm good and ready."

He ran his finger across her lower lip and tangled his hand in her hair. When he kissed her this time it was with barely checked passion. He broke from the kiss and held her at arm's length when he heard Mrs. Fitz come thumping down the stairs.

"Wait until you see the upstairs, Berry. It's wonderful," Mrs. Fitz exclaimed. "You can see forever from the third-floor windows."

Mrs. Dugan followed her. "Not much furniture in this house. No window shades. I can't live in a house without window shades."

Jake gestured to the cartons stacked along the dining room walls. "There are extra linens in one of those cartons. We can tack a couple sheets up for tonight." He zipped his jacket and opened the front door. "I guess I'd better go buy some toothbrushes."

Chapter 4

Mrs. Fitz, Mrs. Dugan, and Miss Gaspich perched on the edge of the couch, their eyes glued to the television set, their mouths slightly open as they watched the last few minutes of *Ghostbusters*. Scattered in front of them were the remnants of supper: Styrofoam hamburger cartons, a few ketchup-soaked French fries, five empty milkshake cups, and a large bakery box containing one lonely doughnut.

Berry sat on the rug, her back resting against the edge of the couch. A gigantic marshmallow man had just appeared on the screen, and Berry decided he didn't seem nearly as menacing as Jake Sawyer stoking the fire in the Franklin stove. Jake wore jeans that seductively clung to the most mouthwatering butt Berry had ever seen. Definitely not the butt of a chemist, she concluded. It would be a sin to hide that butt under a lab coat. Jake Sawyer had the butt of a pirate. A rogue butt. Her eyes glazed over in silent appreciation while she memorized the contours and speculated on the hidden details. When Jake stood and stretched, she quickly transferred her attention to the movie.

She sensed, rather than saw, Jake moving toward her. His knee grazed her shoulder, and Berry knew if she turned her head she'd be staring into the intriguing bulge behind his zipper—the one part of his anatomy that was possibly more perfect than his butt. Don't look! she told her eyes. You know what trouble you got into last time you ogled that bulge!

He nudged her again with his knee, more firmly this time, pushing her forward a bit. "Scoot up," he whispered.

Before Berry knew what had happened she felt him slide behind her, sandwiching himself into a sitting position between her and the couch, trapping her between his legs. She inched forward, but he wrapped an arm around her waist, holding her secure against his chest. His voice hummed softly into her hair. "This is nice."

Nice? Nice was a little bland for what she felt. What she felt was more like *wow* and *holy Toledo.* Unfortunately, this was not the time for *wow* feelings. Her life was complicated enough. She could barely hold her own between the Pizza Place and her studies, and it kept getting worse. First the ladies, then the Jeep, now the fire. Jake Sawyer was pretty darn fabulous, but he was not part of The Plan.

"I don't think this is a good idea," Berry said.

"Shhh, the movie. You'll disturb the ladies."

Berry looked to the ladies but found them engrossed in the heroics of Bill Murray. She wriggled within Jake's grasp, attempting to free herself.

"Lord, Berry, now you're disturbing *me*," Jake said. "Will you stop sliding around? This is going to get embarrassing."

She carefully relaxed into his chest and sat perfectly still, not wanting to encourage anything, but secretly enjoying the intimacy. His steady heartbeat vibrated throughout her body, rain had begun to splash against the dark windows of the cozy Victorian, and the marshmallow exploded.

Mrs. Dugan's eyes shone with excitement as the credits rolled across the screen. "First time I've ever seen that movie. It's a wonderful movie."

Mrs. Fitz agreed. "It was a treat."

Jake eased away from Berry. "Speaking of treats, I have some goodies to distribute."

Two minutes later he returned from the kitchen with an armful of shopping bags.

"Mrs. Fitz, this belongs to you," Jake said, handing her a bag. "Mrs. Dugan, here's your loot." He handed a bag to Miss Gaspich.

"Lipstick!" Mrs. Fitz announced. "He bought me lipstick. And a nightgown." She held it up for inspection. "It's a pip."

"Here's the toothbrushes." Miss Gaspich smiled shyly. "This is better than Christmas. We got slippers, and face cream, and hairbrushes."

Berry looked at Jake. "You're awfully good at buying women's toiletries."

"I have four younger sisters. I know all about girl things," he told her proudly.

Miss Gaspich stifled a yawn, "I can't wait to get into my nightgown and climb into bed." She looked questioningly at Jake. "Where is my bed?"

Jake stuffed his hands into his jeans pockets. "I have four bedrooms, but only one bed. I suppose the most sensible arrangement is for you ladies to use my king-sized bed. Berry and I will sleep downstairs."

Mrs. Dugan narrowed her eyes. "You're not planning any funny stuff, are you? I won't put up with hanky-panky."

"The thought never entered my mind," Jake said. "Berry can sleep on the couch, and I'll rough it on the floor. I have some sleeping bags upstairs."

Mrs. Dugan pressed her lips together. "I suppose that will be all right, but I've got good ears. You better watch your step."

Jake's face creased into a good-natured smile. "Yes, ma'am."

Berry watched the women climb the stairs. "That was really nice of you to get lipstick and moisturizer for them. It's been a long time since they could afford those luxuries."

"You haven't opened your bag."

Berry studied the pale lavender bag on the coffee table. It was smaller than everyone else's bag, and it was from an expensive shop catering to fancy lingerie and expensive perfume. It was a bag designed to hold silk teddies and lacy thongs. "I'm afraid to open it. Is this something extravagant?"

"Sleepwear."

She extracted a small bottle of perfume that she suspected cost more than a replacement for her Jeep. "There's only perfume in here."

"Yup."

"Everyone else got flannel nightgowns."

"Isn't there a nightgown in there?"

Berry searched the tiny bag. "No."

Jake stroked her cheek with his fingertip. His eyes grew dark. His voice turned alarmingly husky. "You're so beautiful with your unruly blond curls and silky peaches-and-cream skin. You should wear nothing to bed but a dab of perfume." His hands traced the slender column of her neck and rested in a caress on her shoulders. "I have a confession to make. I'm in big trouble here. I'm having heart problems."

"Good Lord. What kind of heart problems?"

"Heartache, heartthrob, heart flutters. I feel like the Grinch at Christmas—you know, the part where his heart grew two sizes in one day.

I thought my heart was going to burst when I saw you for the first time, lying on the ground beneath that big old oak tree. You looked like a crazy modern-day wood nymph."

Berry's eyes flew open. "Crazy?"

"For crying out loud, you were flat out on a pizza." He grinned at her indignation and cuddled her close to him. "Maybe someday you'll develop heart problems, and you'll come to me wearing just the perfume."

"Not anytime soon," Berry said. "I have a plan."

"I'm not liking the plan," Jake told her.

He curled his fingers in her hair, holding her head captive while he lowered his mouth to hers and kissed her slowly and gently.

It was like being drugged, Berry thought. Once he was this close to her she was a goner. Her thinking slowed, and her heart rate accelerated. At the first touch of his tongue, her stomach tumbled. He was pressing himself into her belly, holding her against him so she couldn't escape the feel of him wanting her.

"I'm going to tell Mrs. Dugan on you," Berry murmured halfheartedly.

"Mrs. Dugan doesn't scare me."

"Oh, ha!"

"Okay, maybe a little."

There was a pattering of slippered feet upstairs and a fit of obtrusive coughing. "We're going to bed now," Mrs. Fitz called down. "Anybody need anything from the bedroom?"

"Yes," Jake yelled back at her. "Be right there."

Moments later he returned to Berry with two sleeping bags draped over his arm and a large royal-blue silk pajama top in his hand. He dropped the sleeping bags on the floor and held the pajama top up for Berry's inspection.

"My sister Amy gave me these pajamas last Christmas. She has an enhanced image of bachelor existence."

"Mmmm?"

"I'd prefer you wear only the perfume to bed, but if you're the shy type you could start out in these."

Berry took the pajama top and narrowed her eyes. "To begin with, where's the other half? You only brought me the top."

"I thought the bottoms would get in our way."

"Read my lips. I am not going to bed with you."

"You would have if Mrs. Fitz hadn't interrupted."

"A moment of weakness. It won't happen again. And anyway, you don't know that for sure. Maybe I'll just sleep in my clothes."

"Don't you think that will be uncomfortable?"

Berry couldn't think of anything more uncomfortable than sleeping in Jake's silky pajamas. The very idea gave her a lust attack. She chose one of the sleeping bags and laid it the length of the couch.

"They zip together, you know," Jake said.

"Not tonight, they don't."

Jake started to get undressed.

"What are you doing?" she asked.

"Getting undressed for bed."

"Aren't you going to turn off the light? Aren't you going to wear pajamas? Don't you have to brush your teeth, or something?"

"Nope."

"Terrific." She jumped into her sleeping bag and turned her face to the back of the couch.

"I thought you liked watching men undress," Jake said, smiling, enjoying the moment.

Berry grunted and burrowed deeper into her bag.

"Last chance to look," he offered in a loud whisper.

"Oh! Ugh!"

Jake made some chicken sounds, flicked the light switch, and the room was plunged into darkness.

Too bad she wouldn't look, he thought. He was wearing his boxers with the big red hearts and pink cupids. His sister had given them to him as a gag Valentine's Day present, and they'd become his instant favorite. They were awesome.

Berry listened to him position his own bag as close as possible to the couch. There was a rustle of material and the sound of a zipper. In a short time the room was filled with quiet, regular breathing. He was asleep. What nerve! She peeked over the side of the couch and watched him.

He was wickedly tasty-looking, and she had to admit, he really did bring out her voyeuristic tendencies. He also was beginning to bring out other tendencies—like maternal instincts, wifely musings, and lonely dissatisfactions. There was more to this than sex, Berry realized. True, there was an instant magnetism between them, but it would have died a quick death if she hadn't liked him. He was kind. He was fun. He was brave.

She tapped his bare shoulder.

"Mmmm?"

"Jake, are you awake?"

"I am now."

"Why do you want to make love with me?"

There was a soft groan. "You woke me up to ask me that?"

"Yeah."

"I don't know. I guess it's like asking someone why they want to climb a mountain, and they say because it's there."

The instant he said it he knew it was wrong. What he meant to say was that she came into his life and it was love at first sight. And if not first sight, definitely *second* sight. He had no clue where the mountain-climbing thing came from. He must have been dreaming about Everest.

"Jeez Louise," Berry said. "I'm just some mountain to conquer."

"No! That's not what I meant. You woke me up. I wasn't thinking right."

"Me either," Berry said. "Criminy, I'm such a dope." I actually was *liking* this guy, Berry thought. I was getting all gushy inside thinking about us together. And now it turns out I'm a *mountain*!

Jake stared into the darkness. Gonna take some work to dig myself out of this one, he thought.

Slam!

Berry awoke with a jolt and sat up in her sleeping bag.

Stomp, stomp, stomp.

Jake opened one eye and looked at Berry. "We have elephants upstairs? The circus come into town last night while I was asleep?"

"I think the ladies are up."

Jake looked at his watch. "It's five-twenty."

The lights flashed on upstairs, and footsteps sounded on the stairs.

Jake groaned, crawled out of his sleeping bag, and stepped into the clothes he'd dropped on the floor the night before. He flipped the light switch, and Mrs. Fitz stood blinking at them.

She wore her new flannel nightgown and pink furry slippers, and her hair stood straight out from her head.

"Lord," Jake whispered to Berry, "she looks like she's been electrocuted."

Berry bit her lip. "Something wrong, Mrs. Fitz?"

"I need tea." And she shuffled off toward the kitchen.

Next, Mrs. Dugan stomped down the stairs, gave Berry and Jake a cursory glance, and huffed after Mrs. Fitz. There was a flurry of banging pots and clattering silverware from the kitchen. A few minutes later Miss Gaspich joined them.

"Where's the tea bags?" Mrs. Fitz called. "I can't find nothing in this kitchen."

Jake grinned at Berry. "The ladies didn't have a good night."

He sauntered out to the kitchen, and soon soothing sounds drifted in to Berry. Jake was telling Mrs. Fitz how nice she looked in the morning . . . full of energy. Mrs. Dugan and Miss Gaspich were similarly pacified.

Berry joined the group, and a tablecloth

was discovered and spread over the round oak table. A blue teapot appeared. Packing crates were drawn up to serve as chairs. Mrs. Fitz looked like she was beginning to come around, but Miss Gaspich looked like death. Her red-rimmed eyes sagged in her face, and her mouth crinkled into a small furrow in pasty cheeks.

"Miss Gaspich, do you feel all right?" Berry asked.

Miss Gaspich slumped against the table, staring glassy-eyed at her teacup. "Couldn't sleep all night. Didn't sleep a wink."

Mrs. Fitz looked disgusted. "You snored all night, you old bat. And you hogged the pillow."

Mrs. Dugan leaned across the table. "You! You were the one who hogged the pillow. Tossing and turning and complaining. Mildred was the perfect bed partner compared to you."

Jake deposited a steaming mug of coffee in front of Berry. "Looks like we have a problem here."

"Possible multiple homicides."

"I think I'll go out and get some beds today."

He slouched over Berry, draping his bare arm across her collarbone, and whispered in her ear. "I only have four bedrooms. Guess that means two of us will have to double up."

Mrs. Dugan glared at him. "I heard that. You men. You only have one thing on your mind. Sex. Sex. Sex."

Mrs. Fitz winked at Jake. "Don't pay no attention to her. She's cranky because she's always got sex on her mind, too, but she can't remember what you're supposed to do about it. Last man Mrs. Dugan knew was old Criswald, and he couldn't remember what to do about it, either."

Miss Gaspich giggled. Mrs. Dugan looked scandalized. And Mrs. Fitz looked like she was enjoying their reactions.

"I tell you what," Mrs. Fitz said, smiling broadly. "How about when Jake goes out to get us some beds, he gets us some handsome men to go with them?"

Sarah Dugan pursed her lips. "That's disgusting."

"Yeah. But it made Mildred giggle. It's bringing some color to her cheeks."

Berry sipped at her coffee and thought she wouldn't want to underestimate Mrs. Fitz. Her methods were a bit unorthodox for a little old lady, but she knew how to rally the troops.

Jake finished his coffee. "It's Saturday. What time does the Pizza Place open on Saturday?"

"Ten."

"I guess we can get ourselves together by ten."

"First breakfast," Mrs. Dugan said.

Mrs. Fitz drained her cup of tea. "Then the laundry. If we don't do the laundry we'll have to work in our nighties."

Jake set his cup on the table and lazily stretched behind Berry. "I'll take a quick shower, and then we can check out the apartment."

Berry was having a difficult time not bursting into tears. The apartment was even worse than she'd remembered. The soot was everywhere. It had infiltrated every drawer, it clung to the walls, and it blackened the windows.

Jake put his arms around Berry and rested his chin on the top of her head. "It could be worse. No one was hurt."

"Yes, but everything is ruined."

"Not everything."

Berry looked down at the rug. "The rug is ruined."

"Mmmm." His voice rumbled in her ear.

Berry was having a difficult time concentrating on the rug. She was being distracted by his hands inching their way down her spine.

"And the couch is ruined," she said.

"Mmmm. The couch."

The hands squeezed her ever so slightly, and his thumbs massaged little circles into her back just above the waistband of her jeans.

"And . . . um." She couldn't think what else was ruined. It was right on the tip of her tongue, but she was being rendered senseless by his thumbs.

"The curlers were faulty and the company will be responsible for damages, including cleanup," Jake said. "I think we should gather up the clothes and linens and take them all back to my house to be washed. The rest of this you can leave to the professionals."

Berry squeezed her eyes shut and a tear popped out. "It makes me sad to see it like this."

"Me too," Jake said.

"I think I'd feel better if I cleaned it a little."

Jake held her a little tighter. "Me too."

"Really?"

"No," he said, "but I'll do anything to prevent another tear from sliding down your cheek." He turned and rummaged through the drawers by the sink. "Where are your big garbage bags?"

"One drawer down."

He located the bags and tossed them to her. "Here you go. Stuff the clothes and linens in these. I'm going to get the rug up before it ruins the floor."

Berry filled the station wagon with the bagged laundry and looked up at her open windows. Jake was stuffing part of the waterlogged rug through one of them. "Bombs away," he called, catapulting the rug onto the sidewalk below.

"Jake?"

He leaned out the window and grinned. His shirtsleeves were rolled to above the elbow, and a black smudge slanted across his cheek.

"Thanks," Berry called up to him.

"Are you looking for a way to show gratitude?" he asked.

Berry smiled in spite of herself. She had to admire his tenacity.

An hour later Berry returned with Mrs. Fitz and Miss Gaspich. She unlocked the door to the Pizza Place and was relieved to see only a few water stains creeping down the walls.

"Just as good as new," Mrs. Fitz commented.

Miss Gaspich set a bunch of wildflowers on the counter. "I picked these this morning in the woods behind Jake's house. Don't they look nice?"

Berry smelled the flowers. "They look great."

Mrs. Fitz wrapped a snow-white apron around her middle. "We can handle this. You go on upstairs and help Jake with the apartment. Sounds like he's having a party up there."

Berry looked at the ceiling. It did sound like a party upstairs. There was music blaring from a radio and the sound of at least a dozen feet scuffing around. She took the stairs two at a time and found her apartment filled with people. Mrs. Giovanni stood at the sink, up to her elbows in soapsuds. Several adult Lings were scrubbing walls and scouring floors. Ling children ran from bedroom to living room in a game of tag. A tall, rawboned man turned from a sparkling-clean front window. He held a bottle of glass cleaner and looked pleased. "They're pretty clean, now. Now you can see Mama Giovanni's geraniums when they bloom, and down the street my Caribe Restaurant."

Berry caught Jake by the arm as he hauled a load of trash to the stairs. "What are all these people doing here?"

"They just showed up, one by one. You were right. This is a nice neighborhood."

"They came to help me?"

"Mrs. Ling said you were the reason her daughter won her class spelling bee last month. Said you tutored her free for weeks before the contest. Mrs. Giovanni tells me you drove her to the hospital every day for almost a month this winter when her husband had a heart attack."

"The tall man cleaning the windows," she whispered. "I've never met him."

"Apparently you've befriended his wife."

Berry looked confused.

"Anne Marie."

Berry's eyes opened wide. "Anne Marie?" She burst out laughing. "Anne Marie is a six-foot-tall platinum blond who only speaks French. She gets lonely when her husband is at work, so she visits me. I speak English and make pizzas, and she sits on the stool, knitting and speaking French. Neither of us can understand anything the other says."

Jake shook his head. "How can you find time to do all these things, run a business, and go to school?"

"I've eliminated sleeping and only eat once a day."

Jake was serious. "What about time for Berry?"

"I like my life."

"I think you're running on empty. When you say you haven't got time for naked men—you're right."

"Naked men do not play an important role in my life."

Jake grinned down at her. "I intend to change that."

"Good thing for you Mrs. Dugan stayed home to do the laundry. I'd tell her you were talking dirty to me."

"That isn't talking dirty." He leaned forward

and whispered some of his future intentions in her ear. He stepped back, grinning, enjoying the look of flustered embarrassment on her face. "Now *that's* talking dirty."

Mrs. Giovanni bustled past with a bottle of detergent in her hand. She shook her finger at Berry. "You got a nice young man there. You're lucky to have a man like that to take care of you."

Jake whispered in Berry's ear. "See, even Mrs. Giovanni thinks I should take care of you."

"I don't need taking care of."

"Of course you do."

"Not the way you mean."

"Especially the way I mean."

Berry narrowed her eyes and put her fists on her hips. "I guess I know what I need and what I don't need. And I don't need what you think I need. I'm perfectly capable of taking care of myself."

"I suppose you are—but it would be much more fun if we did it together."

"I didn't mean . . . you know perfectly well . . . oh, jeez."

Jake handed her the bag of trash. "Here, this

isn't heavy. It's scraps of wallpaper I scraped off the bedroom wall. You could take it downstairs for me. It'll give you a chance to cool off." He winked at Mrs. Giovanni. "Just being around me gets her all overheated."

Berry took the bag and smacked Jake over the head with it.

Mrs. Fitz stood in the doorway of the Pizza Place and clicked her tongue at Berry. "You look like someone just stepped on your corns."

"It's that Jake Sawyer."

"Isn't he something? Um-hmmm."

"The man has one thing on his mind."

"You?"

"S-e-x."

Mrs. Fitz looked at Berry. "Don't underestimate him."

Berry raised her eyebrows in question.

"He's in love with you," Mrs. Fitz said.

"We hardly know each other."

"Sometimes your heart knows stuff your head hasn't figured out yet."

"He's never told me."

"Maybe he don't know. Maybe he knows, but he's afraid, like you."

Berry squared her shoulders. "I'm not afraid."

"Don't tell fibs."

"It's just that I have this plan."

"Bullshoot."

"Mrs. Fitz! Such language."

Mrs. Fitz laughed and slapped her thigh. "I know it. Aren't I the ornery old lady, cussing like that?" She shook her head and returned to the caldron of pizza sauce bubbling on the stove. "You gotta be flexible, Lingonberry. Sometimes plans gotta change or you lose good opportunities. Isn't every day a man like Jake Sawyer comes along. That man is *fine*."

Miss Gaspich kneaded a huge wad of dough on the butcher-block table. A small smile hovered at her mouth. Her eyes twinkled. "And he's got a great butt," she added quietly.

Chapter 5

It was close to eleven o'clock and Berry's street was dark. With the exception of the bar on the next block, this was an early-to-bed, early-to-rise neighborhood. Berry summoned her last ounce of strength and dragged herself out of the car. She glanced into the window of the Pizza Place, noticing that it was empty, except for Jake. Thank goodness. She didn't have the energy to be nice to any more customers. She pushed through the heavy glass door, tossed the money bag onto the counter, and slumped into a chair. "Another day, another dollar."

Jake gaped at her. "You look awful!"

Berry pointed to her wet ringlets and water-splattered shirt. "Water balloon." She raised her leg to display torn jeans. "Dog."

"Does this happen every night?"

"Some nights are worse than others. Where are the ladies?"

"I sent them home in a cab. They looked all done in." He took her hands and pulled her to her feet. "You look even doner. Let's go home."

"I have to clean the ovens, the floor—"

Jake pointed vehemently. "To the car, woman!"

Berry was too tired to argue. She followed Jake to the car and sat beside him, remembering the way he'd said, Let's go home, as if it really was her home, too. Wouldn't that be nice, she thought, succumbing to the hypnotic drone of the engine. Imagine if that lovely Victorian house could actually be my home. It's nice to see Mrs. Giovanni's geraniums, but Jake's house has trees and a real lawn. She closed her eyes and imagined what it would be like to be barefoot on that lawn. No responsibilities, no plan to follow . . . just bare toes and soft grass.

When Berry opened her eyes she was in the garage.

"Come on, sleepyhead," Jake said. "We're home."

Berry looked at him drowsily. There was that word again. When Jake Sawyer said *home*, it took on spiritual proportions. Home was an ark: a refuge against flood, pestilence, and rude drivers; a haven for the harried; a cure for the sexually deprived.

Berry followed Jake into the kitchen and wondered what it was that made this house so homey. It was empty of furniture. Voices echoed in rooms not yet softened by curtains or carpets. By all standards the old building should have felt inhospitable. But it didn't—it felt like a home. Berry could practically smell butterscotch pudding cooling on the counter.

Suddenly the ghosts of crushed dreams tugged at her heart. Dreams of towheaded children getting tucked into bed at night, dreams of a husband who nuzzled her neck in the kitchen and told her important things, like I took the car to get a new muffler today. She'd entered into marriage anticipating a family, fantasizing about a big old house that would be filled with noisy love and security taken for granted. What a dope she'd been to look for domestic bliss in a marriage to Allen. It had never really been a marriage at all. It had been a living arrangement. She'd expected so much, and she'd left with so little.

She chewed on her lower lip. No, that wasn't entirely honest. The dissolution of her marriage wasn't a totally barren experience. She'd walked out on her emotionally shallow husband with renewed self-esteem and a hard-won sense of purpose. Somehow, an individual had emerged from the muddle of matrimony. She was proud of that.

"Looks like some heavy thinking going on behind those pretty blue eyes," Jake said.

Berry struggled for something to say. "This house feels like it should be filled with children."

"I agree. It's going to be perfect for a pack of kids and a couple floppy-eared dogs."

Berry stared at him in confusion. He didn't have kids, and he didn't have a dog. What was he telling her? Had he bought the house for someone else? An investment? Was he only living here temporarily? Lord, did he have a pregnant girlfriend in Spokane?

Jake leaned against the counter. "I have a plan."

"What sort of plan?"

"When was the last time you ate?"

Berry blinked at the change in the conversation. "I don't remember when I ate last."

"Did you have supper?"

Berry'd had a candy bar for supper. She'd intended to have a sandwich, but somehow she'd never gotten to it. "What's this got to do with your plan?"

"Nothing. Everything." Jake opened the refrigerator door. "There's not much food in here."

"So, I'm not the only one who forgets to eat."

"I've been eating out. Mostly at my sister's house. She's only a few miles from here." He put a half gallon of milk on the counter and found a box of raisin bran in the overhead cupboard. "I've only got breakfast food." He located a spoon and poured her a bowl of cereal.

Berry aimlessly pushed the raisins around with her spoon. "I'm not sure I have the energy to eat this."

Without saying a word, Jake poured some milk into the blender. He added an egg and searched through a small box sitting on the counter, finally extracting two bottles. "A little vanilla, a dash of nutmeg," he told Berry. He whipped the mixture and poured it into a large glass. "Here. You don't have to chew this."

"It has a raw egg in it."

"Eggnog usually does."

"Hmmm." Berry cautiously sipped at it and licked a milk mustache off with the tip of her tongue. He had a plan. Swell. Another plan. The world needed one more plan.

Jake took the empty glass and put it in the dishwasher. He slung an arm around Berry and eased her toward the stairs. "Let's go to bed."

"Don't I sleep on the couch?"

"I had beds delivered today. The ladies all have their own rooms."

"And?"

"And you sleep in my room." He opened the door to his bedroom and motioned her in with a Sir Walter Raleigh flourish.

"Oh, no," she groaned, "not tonight, Jake. I'm too tired."

Jake grinned at her as he turned down the bed linens. "No. Not tonight. When I share a bed with you for the first time I want you wide awake and panting."

Berry stood blank-faced in front of him, too

tired to formulate a retort, her mind focusing on the fact that he'd said *when* I share a bed with you, not *if*. Was it that inevitable?

He draped the royal-blue silk pajama top across her shoulders, kissed her on her forehead, and left, closing the door behind him.

Berry surfaced through the drowse of sleep, stretching her legs, then her arms. She was in the biggest, most comfortable bed she'd ever slept in. "Yum," she sighed, rolling onto her back, feeling the delicious silk pajama top slide over her breasts. This was a lovely way to awaken, she decided. Slowly and luxuriously. If only she didn't have this peculiar feeling of being watched. The feeling crept along her neck and tingled in her scalp. She cautiously opened one eye.

"Morning." Jake grinned down at her.

Berry pulled the covers up to her neck. "What are you doing in here?"

"I need some clothes. Want to take a shower?"

Berry looked at him suspiciously. He had a towel slung over his shoulder. "Aren't you going to take a shower now?"

"Yup. But I'm a good guy. I'd be willing to share it with you."

"What a pal."

"I can do wonderful things with soapsuds."

"I don't think I want to hear this."

Jake sat on the edge of the bed and ran his finger along the blue silk collar. "I like the way you feel under this material. Now I know why they make pajamas out of it. It never felt like this when it was on me."

Berry liked it, too. It was fun to wake up feeling pampered and feminine for a change.

He ran the material between his fingers. "You would feel like this in the shower, when you got all lathered with soap."

Holy cow. No one had ever said anything like that to her before. Not even her ex-husband. *Especially* not her ex-husband!

Jake's desire was obvious in his dark eyes as his finger traced a trail over the small swell of her breast. There was something incredibly carnal about his lazy exploration of her pajama-clad body. She licked her lips in anticipation of his good-morning kiss. When it happened, it said, Good morning, good golly! His hands headed south, and Berry didn't want him to stop. He went from Montana to Salt Lake City and paused at Phoenix. Berry *really* needed him to continue on to Mexico.

"Don't stop," she whispered.

His hands were warm on her belly, his fingertips resting on the thin elastic band at the top of her bikini panties. "Once I cross the border, there's no going back."

Berry exhaled. Crossing the border wouldn't be good. Pleasurable? Yes. Smart? No. There would be no going back in more ways than one. She groaned and pushed away and straightened her nightshirt.

"I need a moment," she said. "It's the first time I've ever felt anything like this."

"You were married for four years. Didn't you ever make love?"

"It turned out that I gave love, and he took love, but we never *made* love. We went through the motions on a regular basis, but nothing ever happened for me." She rolled her eyes. "This is so awkward."

"I hope I never meet this guy. I don't think I could keep from flattening his nose."

"It wasn't entirely his fault. I was very young. Allen and I both thought marriage could be a panacea for our own problems. Allen was very smart. He had direction to his life. He wanted to be a doctor. There I was floundering through school, changing my major every semester, barely passing half my courses—and Allen walked into my life. He was like the calm in the center of a hurricane. Cool blue eyes, perfectly combed hair, always a crease in his trousers. I think, unconsciously, we each felt incomplete. I needed order and purpose, and he was lacking emotion. I suppose we thought if we joined the two of us together we'd get a complete human being.

"Unfortunately, life doesn't work that way. Marriage intensified our problems. The longer we were married, the less sure I became of myself, and he grew more withdrawn, less communicative. When it became clear that the marriage was a failure, Allen began looking to other women for comfort." Berry shrugged. "Maybe cheating was a last-ditch effort for him. Maybe he was trying to convince himself that he wasn't deficient."

"Maybe he was a creep."

Berry hugged her knees and laughed. "That was my original conclusion. Time and personal growth have softened the edges of my animosity."

Someone obtrusively clumped down the hall, stopping short of Jake's bedroom door. "Anyone wanting to use the bathroom should do it now," Mrs. Fitz hissed in a loud whisper. "They should get into the bathroom before Mrs. Dugan gets up!"

Berry was the last to arrive at the breakfast table. She quietly slid onto a packing crate and poured a bowlful of cereal, being careful to avoid looking at Jake. She was practically senseless with embarrassment. She'd gone bonkers listening to him talk about soap. She couldn't have felt more exposed if she'd come to the breakfast table naked. She'd told him her life story. Lord, she was such a boob. She kept her eyes trained on the cereal without really seeing it. She added milk and stirred.

Pow! A kernel of cereal flew past her ear. *Pop, ping, pow.* Her cereal was exploding!

A kernel bounced off Mrs. Dugan's forehead. "I've been shot!" Mrs. Dugan cried. "Someone shot me in the forehead."

Mrs. Fitz dived under the table. "You haven't been shot, you old dunce. It's the cereal."

Jake jumped to his feet and clamped a dinner plate over the almost empty bowl.

"What is this stuff?" Berry asked, her eyes wide.

Jake cautiously removed the plate. The cereal was bloated with milk, making soft snuffling noises. "I don't understand this. It never did this before. Maybe it was the way you were stirring it." He took the box of cereal and Berry's bowl and descended into the basement with them.

Mrs. Dugan shook her head. "This never happened when we lived in the Southside Hotel for Ladies."

Mrs. Fitz picked cereal out of her hair. "Yeah, that place was boring. Filled with old people." She shivered at the thought.

Miss Gaspich folded her napkin. "I like it here. I wish he hadn't taken that cereal away. I wanted to try some."

Berry stared at the cellar door, wondering what was down there. Dr. Jekyll's laboratory? Finally her curiosity grew stronger than her embarrassment. She excused herself from the table and cautiously opened the basement door. "Jake?"

"Mmmm."

"Can I come down? Will anything else explode?"

"Take your chances."

Berry looked around the cluttered, well-lit room. Kites, model airplanes, wind socks, and bicycle wheels hung from the ceiling. The walls were lined with bottle-laden shelves and crowded bulletin boards. Countertops held robot innards, computer equipment, and sacks of rice, whole wheat, and corn. There were toys everywhere: decapitated dolls, fuzzy bears, motorized skateboards, boxes of puzzles. Jake sat at a massive oak desk, intently staring at a soggy particle of cereal speared on a long skewer. Berry moved behind him. "I feel like I'm visiting Gyro Gearloose."

"Most of this stuff belongs to my sister's kids. I'm the toy fixer. The trouble is they break them a lot faster than I can fix them." He looked around the room. "Some of this is mine. The kites and planes and wind socks are mine."

Berry looked sidewise at him. "You told me you didn't have any toys."

"There are all kinds of toys. These are little toys. I didn't think we were talking about *little* toys."

"So you have exploding cereal and a bunch of *little* toys. Are there any other surprises I should know about?"

"I almost never have surprises. My life is an open book."

"Un-hunh."

"Go ahead, ask me anything," Jake said.

"Did you give me that exploding cereal on purpose?"

Jake feigned outrage. *"Moi?"*

Berry sat on a tricycle. "Okay, so go ahead and tell me. What's this big plan you've got?"

Jake leaned forward, resting his elbows on the desk. "We're going to get married, buy a couple dogs, and have a whole bunch of kids. Maybe a hundred. Although I'm negotiable about the kids. One or two would be enough."

"I don't want to get married. Been there, done that."

"Not ever?" Jake asked.

"Maybe someday, but not for years and years."

"I don't want to wait years and years. I'm pretty much ready to get married now. Today or tomorrow would be good."

The man was insane, Berry thought. Fun . . . but insane.

"I have work to do. I don't have all day to stand here and talk about marriage," she told him. "I have to make pizzas. I have to wash the floor. I have to study for an art history test. And by the way, you're a nutcase."

"I'm not a nutcase," Jake said. "I've met a lot of women and I've waited a long time for the right one to come along. And you're the right one."

"How can you be sure?" Berry asked. "How do you know?"

"How long do we have to discuss this?"

Berry looked at her watch. "Seven minutes."

"Not nearly long enough," he said. "You're going to have to go with the short version. I know, because I just know."

* * *

Mrs. Fitz spooned sauce on the pizza rounds laid out on the paddles, and Berry added green peppers, onions, and crumbled sausage. Six large pizzas, always the same, every day, for the lunch buffet at the Hill Top B&B.

"How did you come to live at the Southside Hotel for Ladies?" Berry asked.

"When my Edward died I couldn't see living in our big house anymore, so I sold it and bought a racehorse."

Berry froze in mid-pizza making. "*What?*"

"His name was King Barnaby Von Big Bucks. Didn't seem like I could go wrong buying a horse named Von Big Bucks." Mrs. Fitz sighed. "Just goes to show."

"Why on earth did you buy a horse?"

"I took one of them senior citizen bus tours of big houses with gardens and such. And this one house was a horse farm and one thing led to another and I ended up selling my house and buying a horse."

"Must have been some horse."

"Yeah, he was a beauty."

"What happened?"

"Turned out he was pretty, but he wasn't

real fast. I think that horse *liked* coming in last. I owned him with two other people and they wanted to send him to the glue factory, but I just couldn't do that. So I bought them out with the rest of my house money and gave King Barnaby to some nice young couple that had a lot of land and wanted a horse as a pet."

"And then you were broke?"

"Well, I didn't have my nest egg anymore, but I had social security and some money from Edward's pension. It was enough to pay for my apartment but not enough to buy one of the new condos. And what with the cost of living now, it's hard to find another apartment I can afford."

The door to the pizza shop opened and a rangy, scraggly-bearded kid strolled in. Berry assessed him at late teens. He was wearing a lumpy, wrinkled raincoat and a navy knit hat over brown, shoulder-length hair. It was midmorning and not a lot of people came in for pizza midmorning.

"Can I help you?" Mrs. Fitz asked.

"Maybe," he said.

His eyes darted around the room, taking in the ovens and the workstation and the three small tables with chairs for walk-in customers.

"We don't have any pizzas for take-out made up yet," Mrs. Fitz said. "But we'd be happy to take an order."

The kid took a semiautomatic out of his raincoat pocket and pointed it at Mrs. Fitz. "How about you just empty your cash register," he said.

Berry and Mrs. Fitz froze.

"Now!" he said.

Berry carefully moved to the cash register. "We haven't got much money," she said to him. "We just opened up."

"Whatever," the kid said. "Just hand it over."

"Honestly," Mrs. Fitz said to him. "Don't you have anything better to do than to rob two women? You should be ashamed."

"And you should be dead," the kid said. "How old are you, anyway?"

Mrs. Fitz narrowed her eyes and gripped the sauce ladle. "I'm not too old to take care of you. You need to learn some manners."

Berry had a hundred dollars in twenties and fives in the cash register. She gathered them up and held them out to the kid.

The kid moved to Berry, reached for the money,

and Mrs. Fitz whacked him on his head with the sauce spoon. Pizza sauce splattered everywhere, and the kid's eyes went blank for a moment. Mrs. Fitz gave him another klonk on the head, and he staggered back and dropped the gun.

"Are you okay?" Mrs. Fitz said to him. "I didn't mean to hurt you."

The kid shook his head and looked at his hand. "I'm bleeding. You just about killed me." And he turned and ran out the door and down the street.

"It was pizza sauce," Mrs. Fitz said.

Berry dialed the police and reported the attempted robbery.

"They're sending someone over," she told Mrs. Fitz. "Lock the door until the police get here and leave the gun on the floor. And don't tell anyone else about this." Especially don't tell Jake, she thought.

It was ten o'clock at night and Berry and Jake sat in the dark, looking out the window of his station wagon.

"I'll be right back," Berry said. "This is the last pizza of the night. As soon as I get this sucker delivered we can go home."

"Sit tight," Jake said. "I'll deliver it."

"Thanks, but I've got it."

"The hell you do. I'm delivering this pizza."

"It's my job, my Pizza Place, my pizza."

Jake looked at the dingy yellow brick apartment building. "It's late, and that's a four-story walk-up in a lousy neighborhood. I'm not going to sit here cooling my heels while you're in some dark hallway quietly getting mugged."

"I've delivered pizzas here before."

"Good. Now it's my turn," he said, grabbing the pizza box. "Lock the doors when I get out."

Berry grabbed the other side of the box and tugged. "You'll deliver this pizza when pigs fly."

Jake gasped and looked out the window. "Look at that!"

Berry strained to see. "What?"

Jake jumped from behind the wheel with the pizza and slammed the door shut behind him. "Flying pigs," he called to Berry.

Berry narrowed her eyes. "Son of a beet!"

She stomped into the building and climbed the stairs, catching Jake on the third floor.

"I hate being told what to do," Berry said to

Jake. "Nobody can tell me what to do. This is my business. That was my pizza."

"After we're married this will be a community property pizza. You might as well get used to it."

"Read my lips. We're not getting married."

"You'll come around," Jake said, knocking on an apartment door.

"If I wasn't so tired from all those stairs, I'd kick you in the knee," Berry said.

The door opened and an old guy with a lot of tattoos and gray hair tied back into a ponytail looked out at them. "What is this, tag team pizza delivery?"

"She's crazy about me," Jake said to the old guy. "Follows me everywhere. That'll be ten bucks for the pizza."

The guy handed the money to Jake. "I should have problems like that," the guy said.

"It's not as good as it looks," Jake told him. "She snoops in men's windows and once she smashed my pizza."

"She don't look violent," the guy said.

"Looks can be deceiving."

Berry turned on her heel and stomped down

the stairs. She was all the way to the foyer before Jake caught up with her.

"That was embarrassing," Berry said to Jake.

"Yeah, but he gave me a nice pity tip," Jake said. "We might have something here." Jake opened the downstairs door and stared at the empty street. "Where's the car?"

It was almost one o'clock in the morning when Jake and Berry trudged through the front door of his house. They silently made their way to the kitchen and began fixing a midnight snack of gigantic proportions. They carried the contents of the refrigerator to the round oak table and in the silvery light of moonbeams scoffed down pickles, sandwiches, ice cream, potato salad, and a pint of strawberries.

Jake pushed back from the table while Berry picked at the last strawberry.

"It's okay," Jake said. "I'll rent a new car in the morning. The police were pretty reasonable, considering that's the second car we've had stolen in less than a week."

"In less than a week I've squashed a Jeep, I've had two cars stolen, and my apartment's been

111

charbroiled." And I've almost been robbed at gunpoint, she silently added. "Do you think someone's trying to tell me something?"

Jake shrugged. "That's just the negative side. What about the plus side?"

"What have I got on the plus side?"

"Our friendship."

Berry's heart got happy. Jake Sawyer thought their friendship was important. Imagine that. He liked her! He really liked her. She thought about their earlier conversation in the basement and his cavalier assumption that they'd get married. Was he serious? She rolled her eyes. Of course not! You don't just come out and announce to a woman that you're going to marry her and have a hundred kids and community property pizza. Besides, he'd had plenty of time to continue the conversation in the car on the way back to his house, but he'd never raised the subject. A wave of disappointment washed over her. Oh, great, she thought with a grimace. Disappointment. I'm in big trouble here. My emotional clock is not in tune with my plan.

She would have to be strong. She would refuse to fall in love—and if she already was in love she would refuse to admit it. What she needed was some good old-fashioned hostility. A mean streak to cover up all those cozy feelings.

Jake took her hand in his and tenderly kissed the inside of her wrist.

Berry snatched her hand away. "Don't kiss my wrist."

"Okay. What would you like me to kiss?"

"I don't want you to kiss anything."

"What a load of baloney." He took her hand back and kissed the soft center of her palm. "How about if I kiss your—"

"Don't you dare!"

He sucked on the tip of her index finger. "Can I kiss it in the shower?"

"We're not taking a shower. Stop that!" She swallowed hard when he resumed the sucking, this time touching his tongue to the tip of her finger. She bopped him on the side of the head with a bag of bread. "I said stop that."

"Playing hard to get, huh?"

"I'm not playing anything." Berry stood at the table. "You're going to have to go home."

"I am home."

"Oh, yeah. I forgot." She carted the pickle jars

and packages of lunchmeat to the refrigerator, feeling like the village idiot. She wasn't good at this sort of thing. She was too inexperienced, too overwhelmed by his sexuality, too easily flustered by her own attraction to him.

Upstairs a door creaked open, and one of the ladies padded down the carpeted hall to the bathroom.

Jake put the last of the dishes in the dishwasher. "I'll bet you a dollar it's Mrs. Dugan. I can tell by that authoritarian *thump, thump, thump* of her slippers."

"Mrs. Dugan's keeping her eye on you."

"I know. She has her radar tuned to the sound of lips meeting." He pulled Berry into the circle of his arms. "I think we should put it to a test. Let's see how fast we can get Mrs. Dugan out of the bathroom."

She really shouldn't be kissing him, she thought, but this was sort of a scientific experiment. Who was she to stand in the way of science?

"This is the first of the good-night kisses," Jake told her. His warm lips brushed hers, and his hands splayed across her lower back, press-

114

ing her gently into him. When he spoke, his voice whispered into her mouth. "There are all kinds of good-night kisses. There are good-night kisses when you're done making love and you know it's been a very special night." He kissed the sensitive spot just below her ear and moved his hand to her breast. "And there are good-night kisses that are the prelude to making love. Kisses that are hungry and impatient." His hand tightened slightly.

The bathroom door opened and feet traversed the upstairs hallway, stopping at the head of the stairs. "Somebody down there?"

"It's just us, Mrs. Dugan," Jake answered. "We were having a bite to eat before coming to bed."

"It's late. It's time nice young ladies were in bed."

"I'm trying," Jake sighed.

"Alone!"

"Why couldn't you adopt a bunch of old ladies who were hard of hearing?" Jake asked Berry.

Berry smiled in spite of herself. "And then there are good-night kisses that simply say, Good night."

Chapter 6

He was doing it again. He was dressing in front of her. The man was a flaming exhibitionist. Berry huddled under her covers and listened to the sounds of buttons and zippers. He had no modesty. He had no scruples.

"Aren't you dressed yet?" she asked.

"Why don't you come out from under those covers and find out?"

Berry didn't have to come out from under the covers. She knew he wasn't dressed. She could tell by the goose bumps on her arm. Damn him, anyway.

"Why do you have to get dressed in my room?"

"Because this is my room, too. Because this is where my clothes are. Because there are little old ladies occupying both bathrooms, and I'm in a hurry this morning. Because I get my kicks this way, and with Mrs. Dugan around kicks are hard to come by—you have to take them when you can." He pulled the covers back and kissed her forehead. "You should have looked. It would have been a lot more fun."

He was wearing gray slacks, and a blue button-down shirt. Berry watched him move to his closet and select a tie from a well-stocked rack. "Did you really want me to look?"

"Uh-huh."

"You would have been the only one undressed. Wouldn't you have been embarrassed?"

"Yeah. That's the fun part. You know what happens when men get embarrassed? They get—"

"I know what they get. And you'd better not!"

He gave his tie a small tug and turned to face her. "What do you think? Do I look like a first-grade teacher?"

Berry thought he looked more like a fully clothed model for a Chippendale's calendar. She sat up in bed and told her heart to stop jumping around like that. He was just a man, for goodness' sake. An ordinary man wearing a pair of pants that were perfectly tailored across his slim hips and nifty butt. An ordinary man wearing a shirt that was exquisitely cut to fit luscious broad shoulders and a just-right muscled chest that tapered down to a hard, flat stomach. Why on earth was she getting so tense over this ordinary man?

Because he wasn't ordinary. He was totally delicious and she should have looked. She was a fool not to have looked. After all, she had already seen almost all of him. There was only about five or six inches left to her imagination. The memory of those six inches could probably have carried her through old age. She stared at him in her best attempt at unblinking serenity.

"You look very nice," she said. "Any first grader would be proud to have you for a teacher."

"Thanks," he said. "I have to run. I've called the rental agency. They're sending a car around for you to use. Should be here by eight o'clock."

A cab beeped in the driveway. Jake took keys and loose change from the bureau top and grabbed a navy blazer from the closet.

Berry listened to him bound down the stairs and out the door. She sprang from her bed and rushed to her window for one last glimpse of him. Too late. He was gone. He was dressed. "Dammit," she whispered, "I really should have looked."

She was still thinking about it at the breakfast table when she noticed an unusual silence. Everyone was watching her.

"Something wrong?" Berry asked.

"No," Mrs. Fitz said.

"Nothing?"

"Uh-uh. Nothing wrong with me," Mrs. Dugan said.

Berry looked at the clean teacups and unused cereal bowls. "Not eating?"

"Maybe later."

"In a minute."

"Not just yet."

"Not even tea?" Berry asked.

Mrs. Fitz fidgeted in her seat. "Well, we brewed some. We just haven't gotten around to drinking it yet."

Berry poured herself a bowl of cereal and reached for the milk. She stopped short. "Oh."

"Something wrong, dear?"

"No. Of course not." She stared at the milk carton. She stared at the cereal. It looked like raisin bran. She gently pushed the raisins around with the tip of her finger. She raised her eyes to the three women. "Looks like raisin bran."

"Yes."

"I thought so, too."

"Uh-huh."

Berry sniffed at the bowl. "Smells like raisin bran."

"Does it?"

"That's good."

Mrs. Fitz narrowed her eyes. "Okay, pour the milk in."

Berry pushed the bowl over to her. "*You* pour the milk in."

Mrs. Fitz pushed the bowl back. "Not me. No way. No, sir. Took me half an hour to get the cereal out of my hair yesterday."

Berry compressed her lips. "This is ridiculous. This is just plain old raisin bran." She moved her seat back a few inches and dribbled some milk into her bowl. Nothing happened.

"Stir it," Mrs. Fitz suggested.

Berry stirred it. It didn't crackle or pop. It didn't fly out into space. It didn't even bloat. "Raisin bran."

Mrs. Fitz filled her bowl. "Thank the Lord, I'm so hungry I could eat a horse."

Miss Gaspich served tea, and all three women sipped timidly.

"Tastes like tea," Miss Gaspich offered.

Mrs. Dugan agreed.

Mrs. Fitz swallowed a spoonful of cereal. "Don't know whether I'm relieved or disappointed, but I'll tell you one thing. Tomorrow morning I'm getting up in time to have breakfast with Jake. From now on he eats everything first."

Berry ladled a generous helping of tomato sauce onto a pizza round and covered it with mozzarella. She drizzled a smidgen of olive oil and fresh basil across the masterpiece and looked up as the front door swung open and Jake sidled through carrying two grocery bags. He was followed by an elderly man, also carrying a grocery bag. From the corner of her eye Berry saw Mrs. Fitz wipe her hands on her apron and pat her hair into place.

"Bandit at six o'clock," Mrs. Fitz whispered, "I'm going in for the kill."

"Mrs. Fitz, you've been watching too much television."

"Movies. Isn't that Brad Pitt a honey?"

Jake set the bags on the counter and extracted four plastic cartons containing salad. "Where's Miss Gaspich and Mrs. Dugan?"

"Their night off."

Jake pulled a stool up to the counter. "Here you go, Harry. We're missing two ladies. Guess you'll have to eat lots of salad." Jake made a sweeping gesture with his hand. "Berry and Mrs. Fitz, I'd like you to meet my good friend Harry Fee."

Mrs. Fitz held out her hand. "My name's Lena. Here's a fork. You want to go to the movies later?"

Berry raised her eyebrows at Jake. "I'd like to see you back by the refrigerator, please."

Jake brought a bag with him and haphazardly transferred food from the bag to the refrigerator.

"What do you think you're doing?" Berry whispered.

"Putting the food away."

"I don't mean about the food. Wait a minute, why are you putting all this food in here? Yogurt? Oranges? Is this tuna salad?"

"You never eat anything. When the ladies were upstairs they made you come up for supper. Now that they're at my house you make do with candy bars."

"Who told you that?"

"I have my sources."

"It's a lie. I take good care of myself . . . most of the time," Berry said.

"Nobody could take care of herself with the schedule you're running. You're suffering from too little time and too little money. You study for school while you roll out pizza dough, and you're wearing running shoes that are held together with surgical tape because you're trying to save money to buy a new Jeep. If that isn't enough, you constantly let your heart rule your head. The ladies are lovely people, but they require naps, they can't drive, they can't deliver." He paused and looked longingly at Berry's mouth. "They can't kiss."

"Of course they can kiss, and how did we get to talking about kissing, anyway?"

He nibbled on her left earlobe. "You have this erotic effect on me." He kissed the pulse point in her neck. "It's become an obsession. All I ever think about is kissing you. Well, that's not totally honest. I think about doing other things to you, too, but they're related to kissing."

"Get serious."

His knee nudged against the inside of her thigh. "I'm trying. You're not cooperating."

Berry tried to concentrate, but for the life of her she couldn't remember why they were back there, standing against the refrigerator. It might have something to do with tuna salad. No, she thought, that's not it.

Mrs. Fitz bustled around the front of the shop. She gave Harry Fee a Coke and a hot piece of pizza. "We'll have to go to the late show," she told Harry. "I have to help Berry until the place closes."

Jake nuzzled Berry's hair and molded his hand to her hip. "That's okay, Mrs. Fitz, I'll help Berry tonight."

Berry wriggled away. "No!"

"Yes." Jake was firm.

"You helped me last night and the stupid car got stolen. I don't want your help. You're nothing but a pain in the neck."

Jake put his arm around her and kissed the top of her head. "She's crazy about me," he told Harry. "But she's shy. You know how women are."

Mrs. Fitz got her sweater and her purse. "She's a ninny," she mumbled to Harry. "Don't know opportunity when it comes knocking."

Harry smiled. "I bet you don't pass up any opportunities, Lena."

"Not if I can help it. Trouble is, opportunities don't come along often enough."

Harry held the door for her and winked at Jake. "Don't wait up."

Berry narrowed her eyes. "What did he mean by that?"

"He meant they're going to have an enjoyable evening at the movies, and we shouldn't wait up."

"That dirty old man has designs on Mrs. Fitz," Berry said.

"I don't believe this. You're doing a Mrs. Dugan."

"If anything happens to that dear, sweet old lady, I'm holding you personally responsible."

"Are you kidding me? I'm worried about Harry."

Berry took several pizzas from the oven and shoveled them into boxes. "Is he a really good friend? How long have you known him?"

Jake looked at his watch. "Forty-five minutes."

"What?"

"I met him in the supermarket. Actually, I had him lined up for Mrs. Dugan. Guess I'll have to go back to prowling the frozen food section tomorrow. Frozen food is a good place to meet old guys."

"You purveyor!" she sputtered, wide-eyed and furious. "I know what you're up to. I'm not stupid. You're getting rid of my ladies. You're getting them out of the house so you can talk about soap!"

"Yup."

"You admit it?"

"Yup."

"That's despicable."

He slouched casually against the counter, hands in his pockets. "Mrs. Fitz and Mrs. Dugan and Miss Gaspich are three terrific ladies. They're bright and lively and lonely. It doesn't take a genius to figure out that they'd like some male companionship once in a while. And it doesn't take a genius to figure out that I'd have to be Houdini to get you into bed with Mrs. Dugan around. I think I've reached a creative solution to everyone's problem."

Berry turned on him. "It's not the ladies who are the problem. *You're* the problem. You're ruining my plan. I don't want a relationship. I don't want your tuna salad. I was doing just fine until you came along. For the first time in my life I knew where I was going. I had goals, direction, purpose. I had self-esteem. Now I don't know what I have. Now I have hot flashes and uncomfortable cravings."

Jake looked outrageously pleased at that. "Really?"

"I don't need uncomfortable cravings. I need to study my art history. You can understand that, can't you?" Berry pleaded.

Jake took a step toward her. "What sort of cravings?"

"None of your business."

"Ah, but it is my business." He stood so close Berry could feel the warmth from his body swirl around her. "I feel an obligation to take care of these uncomfortable cravings."

He didn't understand, Berry thought sadly. She had plenty of the type of cravings he was referring to, but they weren't the ones that scared her. It was the pudding cravings, and the baby cravings, that turned her stomach into a churning turmoil. It was the way she felt when she did his laundry and found herself fondling his clean white sweat socks, worrying if they were soft enough, white enough.

"Right now I'm going to take care of the food craving," Berry said, digging in to her salad.

"It's a start," Jake said.

Rain slashed down the plate-glass windows of the Pizza Place, casting the small shop in funereal shadow. The ovens were warm against Berry's back, but the fluorescent lighting did nothing to dispel the gloom of cold April showers.

The front door swung open and two bedraggled men entered, stomping the rain off their sneakered feet. Their first reaction was to sniff the air and smile appreciatively.

"Lady, if I were you, I'd move my bed down here. The pizza smells great."

Berry handed them each a slice on a paper plate. "Are you done? Is my carpet all installed?"

"Yeah. Boy, I was never so glad to be done with a job in my life. Nothing personal, but your apartment really stinks."

"There was a fire," Berry said. "And it's just been painted."

"What kind of paint did you use? That place smells like old socks."

The second man shook his head. "Worse than old socks. That place smells like *dead* socks."

Berry looked at Miss Gaspich and Mrs. Fitz. "Maybe I'd better go investigate."

She and Jake had checked on it this morning, and it had definitely had a strong paint odor. She hadn't been able to open the windows because of the rain, but she'd assumed the fumes would have dissipated by now.

When she reached the top of the stairs her eyes began to sting. Paint, new carpet, dead socks. They were right. It smelled bad, really bad. Worse than this morning. The walls were eggshell white, and the insurance had paid for not the best but not the worst grade of beige wall-to-wall carpet. The windows were sparkling clean. There was insurance money for new curtains and a new couch but no time to shop for them.

She turned at the sound of footsteps on the stairs and smiled at Jake before he pulled her to him and kissed her hello. Just as he always did. As if they belonged to each other, she thought. Casual husbandly kisses. Hello, good night, good morning.

Jake wrinkled his nose. "What's that smell?"

"It's my apartment," she said, moaning. "How am I going to live in this?"

"Don't worry. It's probably just a combination of fresh paint and new carpet. It'll be better in a few days."

Berry felt like screaming. In a few days

she'd be a babbling, drooling idiot. She needed to get away from Jake Sawyer. She needed to get out of his bed, out of his house, away from his shower. Especially his shower. A morning shower used to be a wake-up ritual. Now it was an erotic experience that brought her to the breakfast table cracking her knuckles, wondering if Jake was really as good with soapsuds as he claimed.

Jake looked down at her. "You have a peculiar expression on your face. Sort of desperate."

Desperate. The perfect word. She turned from him so he wouldn't see the fib. "Not desperate. Just disappointed. I'd hoped to move in tonight."

"Obviously that's out of the question. Looks like you're destined to stay with me a little longer," he said cheerfully.

"Maybe it'll smell better tomorrow."

"I doubt it. Not if it keeps raining, and you can't open the windows."

"You seem awfully pleased about all of this."

"I like having you in my bed . . . even if I'm not there with you."

Berry was sure her heart stopped beating. It went *thud* and then there was nothing but singing. Julie Andrews singing that song from *The Sound of Music*. Plus the Hallelujah Chorus. Sometimes Jake Sawyer said things that knocked Berry off her feet. And truth was, Berry liked being in his bed, too. She liked imagining him next to her, his arm possessively curled across her chest, his lips pressed against her shoulder.

"Admit it," Jake said. "You like being in my bed."

"It's very comfy."

"And what else?"

"Nice sheets."

"What about me? Don't you wonder what it would be like to have me in bed next to you?"

"Never. Absolutely never. And stop grinning like that."

"Sometimes you're such a goose," he said, draping his arm around her, ushering her down the stairs. "So, how are you and Mrs. Dugan doing today? Selling lots of pizzas?"

"Mrs. Dugan isn't working today. Miss Gaspich is working today."

He stopped and grasped her shoulders. "Are you kidding me? I asked Mrs. Dugan at the breakfast table, and she said this was her shift."

"She decided to trade with Miss Gaspich. It had to do with irregularity, I think."

"How could she possibly have irregularity? We've got stewed prunes, prune juice, dried prunes, and bran nuggets."

"I'm afraid to ask why you're so concerned about Mrs. Dugan's work schedule."

Jake removed his slicker and wrapped it around Berry's shoulders. He opened the downstairs door and gave her a push into the rain. "Run for it."

Miss Gaspich didn't bother to look up when Berry and Jake burst into the store. She was instructing a burly elderly gentleman in the art of pizza making. "My goodness, you're good at this," she murmured to him.

"Used to be a cook in the navy. And then when my hitch was done I was a butcher. Ran my own shop for forty years, until I retired seven years ago." He shook his head. "Should never have retired. Life is damn boring. The wife and I were going to travel, but she died before we did much of anything."

"I'm sorry," Miss Gaspich whispered.

He made a dismissive gesture with his hand. "It's okay. We had a good life together."

Berry glared at Jake. "You've done it again."

"He was supposed to be for Mrs. Dugan."

"You were going to fix Mrs. Dugan up with a man who has a tattoo on his arm?"

Jake grinned. "It's an anchor."

Miss Gaspich slid the pizza into an oven and waved to Berry. "This is William Kozinski. I was showing him how to make pizza."

William Kozinski extended his hand. "Bill. I'm Jake's friend."

Berry looked at him through slitted eyes. "Of course you are."

"Everyone wants pizza delivered tonight," Miss Gaspich said. "No one wants to go out in the rain."

Jake balanced the boxes in his arms. "Come on, Berry. You drive. I'll deliver."

Berry looked around. "Where's Mrs. Fitz?"

"She just left." Miss Gaspich beamed. "She had a date!"

Bill held up his large butcher's hand. "Don't worry about a thing. Mildred and I can handle things here. You young folks go off and do your deliveries."

Berry turned to Jake. "I'm not leaving this geriatric Lothario alone with my cash register," she whispered.

"He's my sister's father-in-law."

"Oh."

Berry slid behind the wheel and turned the key. Rain buffeted the car and dark clouds roiled overhead. "Where's the first delivery?"

"Sudley Road."

Berry faced him. "Sudley Road? That's pretty far away. Don't we have anything closer?"

"Nope."

Another one of those nights, she thought, sighing. It was hard to make money when she was driving all over the county. In fact, the profit on these nighttime deliveries was marginal once she surpassed a three-mile radius. Heat from the pizzas drifted forward, warming Berry's neck, and the cozy aroma of fresh-baked dough filled the car.

Jake relaxed in the seat next to her, content

with his role of riding shotgun. Berry watched him from the corner of her eye and thought that sometimes life was very comfortable with Jake. There wasn't the need to fill every moment with chatter. In fact, if she had to analyze her feelings for him, she would have to admit to feeling . . . married. It was especially disconcerting since she had been legally married to Allen for four years and never once felt this companionable affection. Life was strange, and there was no accounting for emotions. Emotions went their own way willy-nilly, without consulting The Plan.

Jake sat up straighter as they turned onto Sudley and checked the house numbers. "The white ranch on the left." He grabbed the pizza box and splashed his way to the front door. By the time he got back he was soaked.

Berry grimaced at the sight of his ruined loafers. She should never have let him do the deliveries. He wouldn't accept any pay. Yet every day he came directly from school and worked at the Pizza Place until closing. The fact that she was beginning to rely on his help only compounded her feelings of guilt.

After the third delivery he didn't bother with the hood to his jacket. He couldn't get any wetter. After the seventh pizza he took his shoes off and rolled his pants to midcalf. It was six o'clock and getting dark.

"That's it," he announced, squishing into the car. "I'm going home. I'm not delivering any more pizzas."

Berry looked in the backseat. "We have one last delivery."

"Too bad. Let them eat cereal. I'm cold and I'm wet and this whole thing is stupid. You're not even making any money on these deliveries."

"But I always deliver."

"Not any more you don't. We're going home to talk."

"Just what are we going to talk about?"

"We're going to talk about this pizza business. Then we're going to talk about us."

"There's nothing to discuss. My pizza business is doing fine, and there's no us. What we have is a living arrangement soon to be terminated. I don't mean to sound ungrateful. You've been very kind—"

"Kind?" he shouted. "You think I'm kind?"

"Well, yes."

"I've been kind to your three old ladies, but I haven't been kind to you."

"What have you been?"

"Waiting, mostly. Trying to get rid of Mrs. Dugan. I can't get ten minutes alone with you. The only time we're alone is when we're delivering pizzas, and then I'm busy with my nose in a map or you're falling asleep on the seat beside me. Your lifestyle is not conducive to romance."

"I know that, Sherlock." Berry turned into Ellenburg Drive. "I've told you before. I don't have time for romance."

"Wrong. You don't *want* to have time for romance."

"What's that supposed to mean?"

"It means you're still running scared from your first marriage." His finger lightly stroked her cheek. "Let it go, Berry. Give yourself a chance to fall in love again."

"You don't understand. I have goals."

"You make falling in love sound like a terminal illness."

Berry pulled into the garage and cut the

ignition. "I feel guilty about this last pizza."

"I don't. I'm sure the people who ordered it have already eaten something else. It took us almost two hours to deliver seven pizzas in this damn rain. Let's heat it up in the warming oven and eat it." He opened the kitchen door for Berry and set the pizza on the counter. "I'll be right back. I'm going to take a hot shower and change my clothes."

Berry paced in the kitchen. Jake was wrong. She didn't make herself busy just to avoid romance. Did she? Of course not. But if she did, it was for good reason. She had priorities. She had a plan. Damn that plan. She was beginning to hate it, and it was all Jake's fault. He made her dissatisfied. He dangled all sorts of forbidden pleasures under her nose. For crying out loud, she'd had a hard enough time doing without butterscotch pudding—now she had romance added to her list.

She heard the water stop running in the upstairs bathroom. Jake was done with his shower. She popped the pizza into the warming oven and hastily scribbled a note telling Jake she'd gone back to the Pizza Place to help

Miss Gaspich. Was she running away from romance? Darn right she was.

Miss Gaspich looked up when Berry walked in. "Did you get all the pizzas delivered?" she asked. "I was worried about you out there in this rain. It's a real soaker."

"I was fine," Berry said, "but Jake almost drowned. He's home drying off."

"We didn't have any walk-in business and no new orders so I'm just cleaning up. I'm almost done. Bill is coming over, and we're going out for dessert and coffee. He's such a nice man."

"I know almost nothing about you," Berry said. "You never talk about yourself."

"Not much to tell," Miss Gaspich said. "I was a personal secretary to the president of an insurance company for fifty years. I took the job right out of high school, and when my boss died at age eighty-three I retired. That was five years ago. I gave up my apartment and moved into the hotel for ladies on my pension and small savings. I never thought I'd find myself living in a train station. I suppose I should have put more away for a rainy day, but I always thought . . ." Miss Gaspich gave her head a shake. "I don't know what I thought. I never had a good head for business."

"Never married?"

"No. The right man never came along, and I wasn't the one to settle. I always had a cat."

Berry entered the darkened kitchen on tiptoe. It was twelve o'clock, and if she had any luck at all, no one would wake up. She inched across the floor, waiting for her eyes to adjust to the dim light, and almost screamed out loud when she stumbled into Jake.

His voice was soft and lethally lazy. "It's late."

Berry used to go fishing with her uncle Joe back in McMinneville. They'd sit all day in the warm shade of a willow tree, listening to the hypnotic drone of dragonflies and crickets, and then when she was just about asleep, Uncle Joe's voice would buzz low in her ear. "Well, look at this. This big ol' catfish is finally taking my bait. If we just wait here nice and quiet that fish'll hook himself and we'll have catfish for dinner."

That was the sort of voice Jake had used. A catfish-catching voice.

Berry made an effort to swallow the panic that was rising in her chest. "Miss Gaspich and Bill left early, and I stayed around to tidy up."

His hands were at her neck, massaging little circles. "You feel tense."

You bet I'm tense, she thought. I'm not as dumb as that ol' catfish. I know when I'm about to get reeled in.

She felt his breath whisper through her hair while his hands slid over her shoulders and nestled against the fullness of her breasts. It was an act of gentle possession. As was the taking of her mouth: a silent affirmation of the power he held over her. His tongue touched hers in confident intimacy, and she felt his arousal stir against her belly. She placed both hands against his chest and pushed away. "Lord, you're probably murder on catfish, too."

Even in the dark she could see the look of astonishment on his face. "Catfish?" He rested his head against the refrigerator and groaned. "Do you hear someone at the front door?"

"Miss Gaspich?"

The door opened, and Bill's voice drifted through the dark house in a stage whisper. "Mildred, I had a great time tonight."

Miss Gaspich's answer was low and indiscernible. There was a prolonged silence.

"Holy smoke," Berry said, "you don't suppose they're . . ."

"Sounds to me like he's got a more cooperative partner than I do."

Berry and Jake cringed at the unmistakable *thump, thump, thump* of Mrs. Dugan thundering down the hall, stomping down the stairs. A light flashed on in the living room.

"Mmmmmmmmildred!" Mrs. Dugan pronounced it like a drum roll.

"This is Bill Kozinski," Miss Gaspich said. "We were just saying good night."

"He has a tattoo."

"It's an anchor. He was in the navy."

A car door slammed in the driveway, and Mrs. Fitz and Harry joined the party.

"What the devil is this?" Mrs. Fitz demanded. "Why isn't everyone asleep?"

Mrs. Dugan stood her ground. "You'd like

that. You'd like to have the living room all to yourself, I suppose."

"Darn right. How're we supposed to neck with you standing there gawking at us?"

Bill put his arm around Harry's shoulders. "Time to leave."

They made a quick exit.

Mrs. Fitz glared at Mrs. Dugan. "See what you've done. You made them go away."

Mrs. Dugan shook her finger at Mrs. Fitz. "You'll never catch a man that way. Everyone knows men don't buy what they can get for free."

"Well, that's fine with me 'cause I don't want to be bought."

"Me either." Miss Gaspich giggled. "I don't want to be bought, but I might be persuaded to give it away for free."

Mrs. Dugan and Mrs. Fitz instantly turned scarlet. "Mildred!"

"I think we should all go into the kitchen and make a nice pot of tea." Miss Gaspich smiled pleasantly. "I'm just dying to tell someone about Bill."

Chapter 7

Berry sipped her orange juice and watched Jake from the corner of her eye. He was clearly lost in his own thoughts. He glanced at the clock while he unconsciously drank his coffee. An air of brooding expectancy gave his dark eyebrows an ominous slant. She'd successfully avoided him since the kitchen encounter, trying with little success to sort out her feelings. It was like playing the game of plucking petals off a daisy. Keep The Plan. Junk The Plan. Keep The Plan. Junk The Plan.

In the beginning it had been her body that wanted to junk The Plan, but more and more, it was her mind that wanted to love Jake Sawyer. Oddly enough, he carried a sense of order and security with him. His lifestyle was a little extravagant, what with one-of-a-kind cars and exploding cereal, but his house was a home. That was the part that really scared her. Was she still looking for someone to take care of her mittens? Was she still looking for someone to fill in the blanks in her personality? Jake Sawyer was the man every woman dreamed of, but some incomprehensible, elusive instinct gnawed at her stomach when she thought of commitment to him.

Mrs. Fitz hadn't noticed Jake's preoccupation. She was contemplating the raspberry-colored egg on her breakfast plate. "Looks like Jell-O. Is it Jell-O?"

Jake checked the clock one more time. "Nope. It's not Jell-O."

Mrs. Fitz tried to cut it, but it skittered across the table. "Slippery little devil," she remarked.

Berry had a similar object on her plate. It was green. "You sure this is edible?"

Jake looked injured. "Of course it's edible. It's also entirely natural and high in protein."

"How'd it get green?"

"Spinach extract."

Berry rolled it onto her spoon and watched in dismay as it slithered off Slinky style. "How do you eat it?"

Jake leaned back in his chair. "That's the fun part."

"You have a bizarre idea of fun."

This was better than a room filled with first graders, Jake thought. He got to test out ideas on the ladies. Tomorrow he was going to see what they thought of his dancing Brussels sprouts.

Mrs. Fitz poked the egglike thing with her finger. "Is this a bedroom toy? Is this for those people who spray themselves with whipped cream?"

Mrs. Dugan looked up horrified. "Land sakes, Lena. You're such a pervert. Where do you get these ideas?"

"Well, it don't seem right for breakfast," Mrs. Fitz complained. "At seven o'clock in the morning I don't have the energy to chase my food around."

Miss Gaspich glanced at her watch. "It's not seven o'clock. It's nine-thirty. It's Saturday."

"It don't matter. It's still too early."

Mrs. Dugan looked disdainfully at Mrs. Fitz. "If you got to bed at a reasonable time, you'd be able to get up in the morning. I think it's disgraceful, a woman your age staying out to all hours with that man."

Mrs. Fitz narrowed her eyes at Mrs. Dugan. "What do you mean a woman my age? I'm not so old. Besides, I'm getting younger now that I have a beau. Haven't had this much fun in twenty years."

Miss Gaspich looked happily pensive as she stirred her tea. "I think I'm in love," she said.

Mrs. Fitz shook her head. "It's the quiet ones that fool you. Three dates, and she's goony-eyed."

"Isn't this something," Miss Gaspich said. "Just like the Love Boat where everyone falls in love. Lena and Harry, me and Bill, Berry and Jake—"

"Berry and Jake are not in love," Berry said.

Jake raised his eyebrows.

Mrs. Fitz looked disgusted. "Of course you're in love. Any ninny could see you're in love."

Berry narrowed her eyes and busied herself with her green egg. She held it firmly in her hand and tried to stab it with her fork. "I'm not in love, and Jake certainly isn't in love," she said.

Jake looked at her with amused curiosity. "How do you know I'm not in love?"

"It takes a long time to fall in love. We hardly know each other."

Mrs. Dugan sniffled and stared at her finger-nails.

"Oh, dear," Miss Gaspich said, "I think one of us missed the Love Boat."

Mrs. Fitz put her arm around Mrs. Dugan's shoulders. "Don't worry, Sarah, Jake'll find a man for you."

Mrs. Dugan stiffened her spine. "I don't need Jake to find me a man. If I wanted a man I'd find one myself. It doesn't bother me that I'm the only one here without a boyfriend. Doesn't bother me at all. I found a man the first time around and I can find one now . . . if I want."

"Sarah was married to a wonderful man," Mrs. Fitz said. "And she has a son and two grandchildren."

"You're a big blabbermouth," Mrs. Dugan said to Mrs. Fitz.

"That's amazing!" Berry said. "I had no idea."

"She don't talk about it much because her husband was so sick for so long, and it was hard on the family."

"It was only hard in a financial way," Mrs. Dugan said. "It was hard to make ends meet, but we always managed to find a way."

"What is your son doing now?" Berry asked. "Does he live in Seattle?"

"He's in South Carolina."

"He took up with a floozy," Mrs. Fitz said.

"And I won't set foot in that floozy's house," Mrs. Dugan said. "My son's first wife took a job in Florida after the divorce. She's a nurse at a hospital there. I get nice cards from my granddaughters, but I don't get to see them much being that they're so far away. Sometimes I get invitations, but I know everyone is scraping by, and I don't want to be a burden."

"One of Sarah's granddaughters is enrolled in the University of Miami," Mrs. Fitz said. "She's going into medicine like her mama."

"I'm real proud of her," Mrs. Dugan said.

Jake folded his hands behind his head and tipped back in his chair, looking totally pleased with himself. In fact, Berry thought, he looked downright triumphant.

Everyone jumped when the doorbell rang.

"My word," Mrs. Fitz said, "that's the first time someone's come to the door since we moved in here."

Jake smiled and stood. "Probably just the paper boy collecting."

The four women watched while Jake opened the front door wide to reveal a young man from a courier service. Jake took an envelope from the messenger and waved it at Mrs. Dugan. "It's for you."

Mrs. Dugan covered her mouth with her hand. "Someone's died."

Jake placed the envelope on the table. "I don't think so. The return address is from a travel agency."

Mrs. Dugan still looked worried when she opened it. She scanned the letter, and her eyes opened wide. "I don't understand this. This must be one of those advertising gimmicks."

Mrs. Fitz snatched the letter from Mrs. Dugan. "Lord, we're all sitting here dying of curiosity." Her lips moved while she read. "Sarah, you've won a trip on a cruise ship!"

Berry pressed her lips together and scowled at Jake. "Cruise ship?"

Jake smiled innocently. "Looks like the Love Boat's going to sail for Mrs. Dugan, after all."

Mrs. Fitz continued reading. "It says here this

travel agency is running a senior citizens' singles cruise, and your name was drawn to get a free ticket. All expenses paid. This is real, Sarah. I know about these cruises. They're wonderful. Dottie Silverstein went on one last year."

Mrs. Dugan fidgeted with her teacup. "I don't know. I'll have to think about this. A singles cruise. Goodness."

"You better make up your mind fast. This boat sails tomorrow," Mrs. Fitz told her.

Mrs. Dugan looked at the color brochure that accompanied the letter. "The boat does look pretty. I've never been on a big boat before."

Mrs. Fitz slapped her leg. "Ain't this something? You live long enough and you get to do just about everything."

Mrs. Dugan stood at her seat. "I'll do it!" She placed her hand over her heart. "I have to tell you, I'm scared to death."

Berry looked at the brochure and mentally reviewed Mrs. Dugan's wardrobe. She would need evening clothes, a bathing suit, a couple of casual outfits—none of which was hanging in her closet. The women had been getting by with a bare minimum for years. Their clothes consisted of a few practical dresses and well-worn sweaters.

"I'm going to get another cup of coffee," Berry mumbled.

She took her cup into the kitchen and quietly emptied the sugar bowl she'd been using as a piggy bank. She'd been saving money for a Jeep, but this was an important emergency. She suspected Jake was behind this free ticket and that his motives weren't entirely honorable, but it didn't matter right now. Mrs. Dugan had an opportunity to do something special. Berry counted the money lying on the counter. Almost three hundred dollars. It wasn't a huge amount, but Mrs. Dugan would be able to buy a few pretty things with it.

Berry handed the money over to Mrs. Dugan. "I hereby bestow upon you a paltry sum of money for the purpose of decking yourself out in grand style for this romantic cruise." Berry turned to Mrs. Fitz and Miss Gaspich. "Ladies, you're excused from pizza making for the day. I expect you to chaperone Mrs. Dugan on her rounds of the stores. Don't let her pick up any cute young salesmen. She has to save herself for this cruise."

Mrs. Dugan blushed and smiled. "Well, I might pick up one or two just for practice."

Berry felt the laughter bubbling in her throat. Was this stuffy Mrs. Dugan talking?

Mrs. Dugan hugged Berry. "I know this is Jeep money, and I promise I'll pay it all back. I'll work twice as hard when I come back."

The tears were hot behind Berry's eyes. Mrs. Dugan was suddenly so much younger and happier. It was as if she was a sponge—all dry and shriveled one minute, and then suddenly swelling into radiant plumpness with the promise of a romantic adventure. Why hadn't she seen this? Why hadn't she realized Mrs. Dugan simply needed to have some fun? The answer took her breath away. She'd been so busy depriving *herself* of fun that she'd accepted Mrs. Dugan's stern stoicism as natural.

At seven o'clock Berry turned the sign in the window to read CLOSED.

Jake looked up from the cash register. "Something wrong?"

"We're closing early tonight. We're having a bon voyage party."

Jake put his hand to her forehead. "You running a fever?"

Berry threw her baker's apron on the counter. "Not yet, but the night is still young."

"I like this kind of talk."

"We need party stuff. Chips and dip and cheap champagne."

"I feel like hiring a band."

"I think you've done enough already. After all, you bought Mrs. Dugan's cruise ticket."

"You don't know that for sure."

Berry locked the front door behind them. "Are you going to deny it?"

"No. But I don't think I want to admit to it, either."

"You go across the street to Groman's Bakery and see if you can get some sort of cake. Maybe you can persuade them to write something appropriate on it. I'll get the champagne and munchies and meet you back here."

Half an hour later they rendezvoused at the car. Jake held a large white baker's box in his hands. "Wait until you see this terrific cake. Mrs. Schwartz got mad at her husband and canceled their twenty-fifth wedding anniversary party."

"And you bought their cake?"

"I got a real good deal."

Berry peeked inside. "There must be ten pounds of icing on this cake."

"Mrs. Schwartz likes icing."

Berry slid behind the wheel of the station wagon. "I'll drive, you hold the icing."

Jake settled the heavy box on his lap. "Why did you decide to do this? I was under the impression that nothing short of an invasion by aliens would get you to close the Pizza Place early."

Berry twisted her hands on the wheel. "It was the look on Mrs. Dugan's face. Like she was a little girl, and it was Christmas morning. She hadn't expected anything that nice to ever happen to her again. It made peddling pizza sort of insignificant."

The hand that touched her cheek was gentle. It tangled in the hair behind her ear and caressed her neck. "You deserve nice things, too. If I gave you a cruise, would you go on it?"

"Don't even think about it. No more cruises!"

"Maybe we could go on a cruise for our honeymoon."

"Honeymoon?"

The car careened into the wrong lane and thumped against the curb, causing the cake to fly off Jake's lap, smash into the dashboard, and flip over onto Jake's feet. Berry came to a screeching halt, looking first at Jake's chalk-white face and then at his brand-new loafers, buried under a mountain of icing. Berry clapped her hand over her mouth. "Oh, crud."

Jake plucked a gooey piece of cake from his trouser leg and tasted it. "Not bad."

Berry reached down and lifted a sizable lump from his cuff. "Yum, cherry filling between the layers."

"Mrs. Schwartz knows what she's doing when it comes to ordering cake."

"Ah, about the honeymoon. You did say honeymoon?"

"Mmmm. Remember my plan. Kids and dogs and a wife and stuff? Not necessarily in that order. Man, this cake is great." He offered her a piece from the dashboard. "You have to try this. One of the layers was chocolate."

"Are you serious?"

"Of course. I wouldn't kid about chocolate cake."

Berry felt the cake flipping around in her stomach. "Kids and dogs and wife and stuff?"

"I told you about it in the basement the other day."

"Number one . . . you're ignoring *my* plan. And number two . . . of all the nerve! You just don't *assume* these things. What about a proposal?"

Jake licked the cake from his finger. "If I asked you to marry me, what would you say?"

"No!"

"Exactly. I decided my best shot was to hang around and make myself lovable and indispensable."

She squinched her eyes closed and slapped herself on the forehead. "Unk."

"How do you do that? How do you make that sort of strangled sound in your throat?" Jake asked.

When she stopped the car he was going to find out. She was going to place her fingers on his neck and squeeze until he made his very own strangling sounds. It would be okay. She was sure the judge would understand.

She pulled into the garage and reconsidered the choking idea. Suppose her fingers didn't choke him. Suppose they wandered over his broad shoulders and played with the baby-soft curls of hair around his ears. In the past, her fingers hadn't been too trustworthy. Probably choking was not a good idea. And what about that twinge of excitement that hit her stomach when he said *honeymoon*? In all honesty, before fury there had definitely been glorious delight. Better not choke him—it wasn't good taste to choke someone you might marry. Oh, Lord, did she just think that?

Jake slid his feet out of his shoes. "If I'm careful I can leave most of the cake here."

Berry nodded numbly. She was doomed. A small hysteria-inspired giggle escaped before she firmly clamped her mouth shut.

Jake looked at her sidewise. "Are you laughing at me?"

"That wasn't laughing. That was a temporary loss of self-control."

"Well, at least we're moving in the right direction."

Berry pushed through the kitchen door and set her grocery bag on the counter.

Mrs. Fitz was making tea. "You're home early! Oh, Lord, now what?" she worried. "Another fire? The Pizza Place burned to the ground?"

"I decided to close early."

"You never close early. Something happened and you don't want to tell me. Was it the gas line? Did the gas line blow up?"

Berry took a large bowl out of the cupboard and began filling it with chips. "I just closed early. Boy, you'd think I was some kind of workaholic. You'd think I never closed early before."

Mrs. Fitz gave Jake the once-over. "What happened to him?"

"Cake."

"What were you doing?" she said to Jake. "Eating it with your feet? Is this something kinky?"

"It was an accident," Berry said. "This big cake sort of fell on him." She waved her hand in a dismissive gesture. "Anyway, we're going to have a bon voyage party for Mrs. Dugan. I even bought champagne."

Mrs. Fitz's face crinkled into a smile. "What a wonderful idea. I'll go get Mildred and Sarah.

They're upstairs, fussing with Sarah's new clothes."

A moment later Mrs. Dugan shyly stepped into the kitchen. "Well," she murmured, "what do you think?" She was dressed in a smart navy pantsuit with matching navy shoes and a soft white shirt. Her hair had been cut and waved into a feminine bob that was short enough to show off a pair of small pearl earrings. "I went to the beauty parlor. Do you think that was wasteful of me?"

"Mrs. Dugan, you look beautiful." Berry hugged her. "This is much more fun than buying a Jeep. And the beauty parlor was a great idea."

Jake tucked a bottle of champagne under his arm and arranged five champagne glasses on a tray. "Berry, you get the snacks, and we'll have this party in the living room while Mrs. Dugan shows us her new wardrobe."

Mrs. Fitz settled herself on the couch. "Even the bathing suit. She looks pretty good for such an old bag."

"I'm not so old," Mrs. Dugan told her. "I've kept myself in shape. I'm almost as good as new."

* * *

Berry slouched low in the couch, her legs outstretched, her hand toying with her empty champagne glass. "That was nice," she said to Jake. "It would have been better if we'd had a cake, but it was still okay."

Jake slid his arm around Berry's shoulders. "The ladies are all tucked into bed for the night. I think this is a good time for us to have a serious discussion."

"Okay," Berry said, "but I might need to fortify myself with another glass of champagne."

Jake refilled her glass. "Are you sure you want more? You look a little fuzzy."

Berry chugged the wine and blinked when it hit her stomach. She wasn't much of a drinker. In fact, she wasn't any kind of a drinker. She was strictly root beer and orange juice until tonight. "I'm doing very amazingly at handling my liquor," she said.

Jake grinned. "When was the last time you had a glass of champagne?"

Berry put her finger to her forehead to help herself think. "Hmmmm. It was at my cousin Melanie's wedding. We all toasted the bride, and then I threw up."

"You're not going to throw up now, are you?"

Berry shook her head. "It was food poisoning. The chicken was contanimated." She giggled. "Did I say *contanimated*?" She walked her fingers up Jake's shirt. "You know, you're awful cute. Sometimes I have to sit on my hands to keep from ripping your clothes off."

Jake rolled his eyes to the ceiling. "She's snockered. I finally have her alone, and she's drunk as a skunk."

"You bet I'm drunk as a skunk. Wanna take advantage of me?"

He stared at her.

"Well?" she demanded.

"I'm thinking about it."

"Heavens. What passion."

Jake sighed. "I can't do it."

"Of course you can do it. It's easy. I'll help you." She settled herself in the crook of his arm and snuggled against his chest. "First thing we have to do is get you undressed." She flipped open his top two buttons.

"Stop that! No one's getting undressed," he said.

"Don't be shy. I've seen you in your undress. All but a couple inches."

Jake looked down at her. "Honey, you missed more than a *couple* inches."

"I didn't mean that couple inches. Well, I guess I did, but not in that way. Not extended."

"How about if I make us some coffee?"

Berry opened the last remaining button. "Wow," she said, "what a body. I must have been crazy to think you had a hunchback." She pulled his shirt aside and rested her cheek on his bare skin. "Yum," she purred, stroking the thin line of hair that disappeared behind his jeans. "Just like bread crumbs."

"Bread crumbs?"

"Like in Hansel and Gretel. Remember how they followed the bread crumbs to the gingerbread house?" He felt so good against her cheek, Berry thought. So enticing. "Uh-oh," she exclaimed. "Your pants are blocking the way to the gingerbread house."

"Berry!"

"Yes, Jakey?"

"I think we'd better get you up to bed."

Berry's eyes slid closed. "Not now. I'm too tired."

He pulled her to her feet, but her knees crumpled.

"Whoops," she mumbled, tumbling into him with a thud. "No knees. What happened to my knees?"

Jake scooped her into his arms and carried her to the stairs. At the third step her head bonked against the wall and her foot caught in the polished wooden railing.

"Dammit," Jake swore, "this never happened to Rhett Butler."

"Who?"

He set her down on the stairs and propped her up against the wall while he contemplated the task before him. Finally, he slung her over his shoulder like a sack of potatoes and carted her off to his bedroom.

"Oh, no," Berry groaned, falling spread-eagle onto the comforter, "I've got the whirlies." She draped one leg over the side of the bed until her foot touched the floor. "There, that's better."

"Berry, you can't sleep like that."

"Why not?"

"Because—"

Whump. Berry fell off the bed onto the floor.

Jake pulled her to her feet. "That's why not."

"This is embarrassing. I've never been drunk before. I don't like it. I'm not doing this ever again."

Berry looked at Jake through half-closed eyes. "Is it always this bright in the morning?"

"How do you feel?"

"My eyes feel like two fried eggs and there are little men wearing pointy hats and spiky shoes running around in my stomach."

"Would you like some breakfast?"

"Not a chance."

Jake looked at his watch. "I'm going to have to get Mrs. Dugan to the boat. I'll drop Mrs. Fitz and Mildred off at the Pizza Place. You can take the day off."

"Mrs. Fitz and Mildred can't do deliveries."

"It's Sunday. You don't deliver on Sunday."

"Since when?"

"Since now. It's a new rule I just made up."

New rule he just made up? What a lot of nerve. Now he was making up rules for her business. She sat up in bed. "Listen here, Sawyer . . ."

"Yes?"

Suddenly she didn't feel well at all. The little men in pointy hats were doing strange things in her stomach. She covered her mouth with one hand and threw the covers off with the other. "I'm going to be sick!"

She slammed the bathroom door and sank down onto the tile floor, resting her head against the porcelain tub. Ah, that was much better, she decided. Nice and cool. Now if she could just get rid of the little men in her stomach.

Jake knocked on the door. "Berry, open the door."

"I'd sooner die."

"Are you okay?"

"No, I'm not okay. I'm being sick."

"Can I help?"

"Throwing up is not a group activity."

Several minutes later she draped a wet washcloth across her forehead and opened the door. "I'm going back to bed to die, now. No deliveries on Sunday sounds like a good rule to me."

Jake helped her into bed and tucked the

covers around her. "I'll be back as soon as I get rid of Mrs. Dugan."

"Don't rush. I'm just going to stay here and feel sorry for myself."

Berry poured herself a glass of cranberry juice and stood absolutely still for a moment, enjoying the quiet solitude of the kitchen. Mrs. Fitz and Miss Gaspich were at the Pizza Place, and Jake hadn't returned from the boat. Berry had slept the morning away, and then had stayed in bed for a while thinking about plans.

Plans were only guidelines, she'd decided. They were preliminary blueprints for the real project, and sometimes even well thought-out plans didn't work right. For instance, she was miles deep in love with Jake Sawyer years ahead of time. Why should she be so upset about that? If it turned out she could graduate several years ahead of schedule she'd be ecstatic. Why was falling in love so different?

Berry, Berry, Berry, she warned, you're rationalizing. There is a difference.

Oh, yeah? she answered her more practical self. Shut up.

And then there was this business about butterscotch pudding and Mrs. Dugan. She didn't want to become a Mrs. Dugan. Now that she thought about it, she realized pudding really didn't take all that long to make. Surely she could find ten minutes a week for pudding. Probably she could squeeze a little romance into her schedule, too. Of course, it would be with you-know-who . . . Mr. Yum.

Being miserably sick had at least given her the opportunity to analyze her problems. In the calm aftermath of her first and last hangover, Berry soberly concluded that you could get carried away with deprivation and timetables.

"Down with deprivation," Berry shouted, brandishing a wooden spoon. She finished her cranberry juice and hummed happily as she hunted through the cabinets for pudding ingredients. Cornstarch, brown sugar, vanilla. She took butter and milk and eggs from the refrigerator.

Boy, she thought, life is wonderful. Here I am, happy as a clam, making pudding in Jake's cozy kitchen. She stirred the mixture with a wire whisk while she waited for it to boil. She separated the eggs and measured the butter. Pudding from a box was okay, but it wasn't like scratch pudding. Scratch pudding was buckled shoes and Monopoly.

She was so intrigued with the thickening pudding that she almost missed the sound of the car pulling into the garage. Jake! Her heart skipped a beat. Stop that, she commanded her heart. It's only Jake. He lives here, remember? But she couldn't stop smiling. She loved him totally, truly, passionately, ridiculously. And she wanted him.

She took the pudding off the stove and added the butter and vanilla. Yes sir, this was a much better plan. First, make the pudding. Second, get Jake Sawyer into the sack. Third, have her head examined. She had to be crazy. Most likely it was the alcohol. It had pickled her brain. She'd heard it could do such things.

In the absence of sherbet glasses, Berry poured the pudding into coffee cups. She heard Jake move to the kitchen and knew he was leaning his hip against the counter, his arms loosely crossed over his chest, watching her. She kept her eyes glued to the coffee cups, but she felt him assessing what he saw: Lingonberry Knudsen braless in a skimpy T-shirt and silky little running shorts. She wriggled her bare toes against the tile floor and gnawed on her lower lip. She had a new plan and she was determined to see it through to the end. Now if she could stop hyperventilating and get her blood pressure under control she'd be just dandy.

Jake crossed to where she was working and looked over her shoulder. "Smells great. What is it?"

"Butterscotch pudding." Was that her? All husky-voiced and inviting?

He scraped some pudding off the side of the pot with his finger and took a taste. "It's good!"

"Yup," Berry said. "And I've got something even better . . . soap."

"Soap?"

"Yes sir, soap. I feel like taking a shower with lots of soap."

"Have you been drinking again?"

"Nope. Been there, done that, didn't like it, not doing it again." She put the pudding pot in the sink and ran water into it so it could soak. "Moving on to bigger and better stuff," she said.

She crossed the kitchen, turned when she got to the stairs, and stripped off her shirt. She smiled at Jake and made her way to the land-ing, halfway to the second floor. She paused long enough for her running shorts to hit the carpet. When she didn't hear footsteps behind her, she turned and placed her hands on her hips. "Aren't you coming?"

"No, but I'm very close," Jake said, unbuttoning his shirt as he followed her up the stairs. By the time he reached the bathroom she was already in the shower. He dropped his jeans at the bathroom door, removed the rest of his clothing, and joined her.

"I finally get to see all of you," Berry said, smiling.

Jake returned the smile and took the soap from Berry's hands. "More than a couple inches," he said with pride.

Hours later Jake drowsily opened his eyes and pulled Berry on top of him. "Mmmm," he murmured, kissing her neck, running his hand along the smooth curve of her back. "Holy cow," he exclaimed, looking at his watch, "do you know what time it is?" He moved out from under her and reached for his jeans. "Poor Mrs. Fitz and Miss Gaspich have been stranded at the Pizza Place all day. I should have picked them up an hour ago."

Chapter 8

Berry slumped deeper into the couch and furiously zapped stations with the remote control. "Twelve forty-two," she muttered, glaring at her watch. The ladies were upstairs, asleep. Everyone was asleep but her and Jake. She'd thought it was cute when he'd had a sudden burst of inventive inspiration during supper and gone charging off down the cellar stairs. It had stopped being cute at about eleven-thirty. Now it was downright infuriating. She took a deep breath and tried to calm herself, knowing that she was being unreasonable. For the past two weeks, Jake had given up all his spare time to work in the Pizza Place. He deserved this night to himself. He was a chemist. An inventor. He needed to work at his profession. But why tonight? How could he leave her alone like this after they'd shared such a beautiful afternoon? It was the first time she'd ever really made love with a man, and her world felt tilted. She'd expected his world would be equally tilted.

"It's tilted, all right," she said aloud to herself. "Tilted in the opposite direction from mine. He could hardly wait to get away from me." She gave herself a shot to the forehead with the heel of her hand. "Ugh, men!"

That was a bunch of garbage, she thought. She was letting all her old insecurities come back to haunt her. She shut the television off and crept up the stairs, telling herself that men simply looked at these things differently. They took life in stride. That was the basic difference between men and women. Women were women. And men were thoughtless beasts! Berry wrenched the bedroom door open and closed it with a thunderous slam. She stripped off her clothes and flung herself into bed, covering her head with the pillow. This is just temporary insanity from too much sex, she groaned. I should have started out slowly. And I certainly shouldn't have done it the same day I made pudding. It overloaded my system. I'll feel better tomorrow.

Three hours later Berry thrashed side to side

in bed. She squinted at her clock and muttered an oath. She punched the pillow and viciously kicked at the confining tangle of sheets. You were supposed to be relaxed after you made love, she fumed. You were supposed to go to sleep with a smile on your face. What was wrong with her? She'd made love all afternoon. Why wasn't she tired? Why wasn't she smiling?

Another three hours later Berry half opened one eye and caught Jake tiptoeing around the room, gathering his clothes. "Jake?"

"Sorry I woke you. Go back to sleep," he whispered.

"What are you doing? Why don't you come to bed," she said.

He stood over her with a tie dangling from his hand and a blue shirt thrown over his shoulder. "I can't. I have to get to school early today. If I could just find my damn shoes . . ." He looked under the bed and grunted with satisfaction. "Found them." A quick kiss on the top of her head and he was gone.

Berry stared at the closed door and sighed. She didn't want to be an alarmist, but this was beginning to feel a heck of a lot like her marriage. She slipped into a pair of jeans and a soft flannel shirt and went in search of breakfast.

Mrs. Fitz was already at the round oak table, sipping tea. "Holy cow, Lingonberry, you look awful."

Berry got the coffee brewing. She banged a coffee mug onto the kitchen counter and stared at it.

"Looks to me like you got man problems. What'd that Jake Sawyer do now?" Mrs. Fitz asked.

"Nothing."

"Nothing? Uh-oh. That don't sound good."

Berry propped herself up on the counter while the coffee dripped into the glass pot. "Boy, love really stinks," Berry said to the coffeepot more than to Mrs. Fitz.

"Yeah," Mrs. Fitz agreed, "it can be a bummer."

"Are you in love with Harry?"

"I don't know. It's hard to tell at my age. You don't know whether it's love or just the prune juice working."

Berry poured herself a cup of coffee and set a skillet on the stove. "You like French toast?" she asked Mrs. Fitz.

"Who's making it?"

"I am."

"Yeah. I like it."

Berry cracked three eggs into a shallow dish and whipped them with a fork. "Good," she said, "because I'm going to make a whole loaf of it."

It was eleven o'clock at night when Berry finally drove down Ellenburg Drive and solemnly stared at the house. Lights blazed from the downstairs windows and Jake's car was parked in the driveway. He hadn't shown up for work at the Pizza Place, and he hadn't called beyond leaving a short message to say he was busy. Berry parked and made her way through the house to the kitchen where Jake was hunkered over the table. His shirttails were out and his shoes were kicked off.

"What's going on?" Berry asked.

Jake gestured to the stacks of dog-eared notebooks in front of him. "I'll never catch up. I didn't know I had to grade these things."

"Can't you grade them tomorrow?"

"Tomorrow I have to grade spelling work-books." He thumped his finger on a smudged page he'd been reading. "These kids are really something. They've actually been paying attention to me. I taught them to add!"

Berry had to smile at the pride and astonishment in his voice. "Can I help?"

"No. This is something I have to do myself." He pasted a scratch-and-sniff sticker on the book and moved on to another.

Berry cracked her knuckles and sighed. She emptied the bag of groceries and polished off three butterscotch puddings. "I guess I'll go to bed," she said in a conversational tone to the kitchen.

Neither Jake nor the kitchen answered her, so she kissed Jake on the top on his head and dragged herself up the stairs. He's such a good guy, she thought. He's trying to be a good teacher. Problem was, it felt a lot like Allen trying to be a good doctor. She'd been understanding with Allen, and she wanted to be understanding with Jake. Unfortunately, she needed some acknowledgment that something special had passed between them. She needed reassurance that Jake loved her. And she didn't want to have to beg for it.

The next morning Mrs. Fitz looked up at Berry from the breakfast table and shook her head. "Boy, I thought you looked bad yesterday, but this beats all. Your eyes look like tomatoes."

"I had a hard time getting to sleep."

"Jake didn't look so hot, either. He left about an hour ago with his hair standing on end and his tie hanging crooked."

"He say anything about me?"

"Nope. He just kept mumbling about Joey Barnes and how he was going to flunk math if he didn't learn how to keep his papers neater."

Berry took a brand-new store-bought apple pie from the refrigerator, added three scoops of vanilla ice cream, sat down across from Mrs. Fitz, and dug in.

"You can always count on an apple pie," Berry said.

Berry slammed the front door to the Pizza Place behind her. "That does it. Boy, that *really* does it," she shouted, throwing her books onto the counter. She waved a piece of paper at Mrs. Fitz. "Do you know what this is? This is what being in love does to you. Makes you stupid. Makes you fail art history tests." Berry flapped her arms. "I knew this would happen. I just knew it. There's not enough room in my head to think about both Jake Sawyer and Vincent van Gogh. Ever since Jake Sawyer popped into my life I've been neglecting my studies, and now I'm failing," she wailed. "I've worked so hard for my degree. All down the drain for a few moments of savage passion."

Mrs. Fitz's eyes opened wide. "Really? Savage passion?"

"Savage passion. The whole nine yards." Berry chomped on a bread stick. "And I'm crazy in love with him. Absolutely bonkers." She drew her eyebrows together. "But I'm not going to be. I'm going to fall out of love this instant. I have finals coming up. If I study hard I might be able to pull my grades up." She wrapped a white apron around her waist and set her textbook on the counter.

Berry removed the towel from her head, shook out her damp blond curls, and rolled her eyes at the crashing, clanking sounds originating from the kitchen. Jake must have come home while she was in the shower. Only Jake could make that much noise in the kitchen. He was probably looking for dinner, doing his bear-foraging-in-the-woods routine. Mrs. Dugan was still on her cruise, Mrs. Fitz and Miss Gaspich were at the Pizza Place with Harry, and Berry had taken a couple hours off to try to relax after grinding her way through three chapters on Renaissance art.

Jake's voice carried up to her. "I can never find a damn thing in this house," he muttered. "Nothing's ever in the same place twice." Another volley of clattering accompanied by swearing. "Too many women! All I wanted was a pizza, and look at what I got . . . four women who can't agree where the frying pan should go."

All he wanted was a pizza! That had become painfully obvious during the past week. He hadn't said more than ten words to her since The Momentous Occasion on Sunday. She stepped into a pair of lacy blue panties and tugged at her jeans, silently swearing that she was never going to bed with another man for as long as she lived. She was a flop in the sack, and she had no intention of humiliating herself ever again. She wrenched the jeans over her hips and zipped them halfway. They wouldn't zip any further. "Damn!" She stood tall and held her breath and pulled. She had them zipped, but she couldn't button the top button. A soft roll of flesh hung over the waistband. Berry stared at herself in the mirror. She was fat! She tapped her foot. This was all Jake's fault, the creep. She'd wanted romance, but she'd had to settle for food, and now she was *fat*. Berry gave up on the button and shrugged into a T-shirt, gaping in disbelief as it stretched taut across full breasts. Hot damn. She had cleavage. She tipped her head back and gave herself a critical look. Who would have thought getting cleavage would be this easy? Turned out all you had to do was get fat.

Jake appeared in the doorway. "Having problems?"

"My pants don't fit." She poked at the roll. "I guess this is butterscotch pudding."

"I hope this isn't going to ruin your appetite. I made a great dinner for tonight."

"You made dinner?"

"Actually, I bought it, but I made the money that paid for it."

Berry followed Jake downstairs and they

stopped at the entrance to the dining room and stared in silent horror.

Berry was the first to speak. "There's a dog on the table."

"Dammit, I wanted it to be a surprise."

"You succeeded." Berry looked at the empty serving bowl. "Is this bowl supposed to be empty?"

"It's supposed to be filled with beef Bourguignon. That slob of a dog ate my dinner!"

"And this basket?"

"Used to be rolls in there."

Berry could hardly keep from laughing. The floppy-eared puppy resembled a furry Buddha, sitting in the middle of the table like a centerpiece. It wagged its tail against the white lace tablecloth. *Thump, thump, thump.*

"Hard to believe this little dog could eat all that food," Berry said.

"Are you kidding? Look at that stomach. She looks like a beach ball with legs."

"She ate everything but the peas."

Jake picked the dog off the table and stroked her glossy black head. "I thought she was secure in the carrier the pet store gave me."

Berry bent to retrieve a piece of ragged red cardboard. "You mean this box that's been chewed to shreds."

"Maybe we should name her Jaws." He sat her on the floor and watched her scamper in a small circle. The puppy stopped and squatted.

"Maybe we should call her Puddles."

He ran his hand through his hair. "Oh, man, look at this mess. The only name for her is Calamity Jane."

"Haven't you ever had a puppy before?"

"No. Have you?"

"No."

"It was part of my plan. You know, floppy-eared dogs running around after a pack of kids."

"Lord, you don't have a pack of kids stashed away somewhere, do you?"

Jake grinned. "No. The kids come last. They're the fun part. We get to make the kids."

"We?"

"Oh, gross! Your dog just threw up on my foot. This never happens in the movies. You ever see a dog throw up on George Clooney's foot when he's trying to be romantic?"

Berry looked at Jake suspiciously. "Why are you trying to be romantic?"

"It's the weekend. I'm finally caught up with my schoolwork, and I thought we could get reacquainted. It's been really nice of you to be so understanding," he said, running his hand through his hair. "You can't imagine what it's been like for me to have to sit here grading papers until all hours of the morning. Sometimes I just felt like walking away from it all and climbing into bed with you, but I couldn't do that to those kids."

Here's the thing, Berry thought. I'm going to have to work on trust and patience, and he's going to have to improve his communication skills, or I'm going to end up looking like a blimp.

"Now that I'm caught up, I wanted to do something special for you," Jake said. "A romantic dinner for two, some very private dancing, and some very passionate lovemaking."

"Great," Berry said. "You go upstairs and wash your foot while I take care of this mess."

When Berry had the floor completely clean, she tucked the puppy under her arm and carried her to a grassy knoll overlooking the little stream. A week ago everything had been bleak and brown, but April rains and unusually warm weather had prompted grass to grow and trees to bud. Berry stretched flat on her stomach and smiled. Calamity Jane bounded down a grassy slope, yelped in fright when she confronted a dandelion, and raced back. Berry hugged the little dog. "Would you like to know a secret?" she whispered. "I've always wanted a little black dog with floppy ears."

The puppy looked like she might explode with happiness. She furiously wagged her tail and rolled on her back. When she spied Jake coming out of the house she rushed up the hill to greet him.

Jake set a cardboard box on the ground and spread a white linen tablecloth next to it. "The alternate plan for the evening is an exotic, romantic picnic." He placed two crystal goblets on the tablecloth.

Berry skeptically looked at the bottle in his hand. "Champagne?"

"No. I decided to play it safe and go with sparkling apple cider." He added two sterling silver candlestick holders with lavender tapers, lavender linen napkins, two white-and-gold china plates, and a silver tray stacked with elaborately decorated petits fours. He plunked a foil-wrapped package on each of the Lenox plates. "Peanut butter and jelly," he explained. "My specialty."

"Good. I love peanut butter and jelly."

Jake lit the candles and leaned back on one elbow to watch the sun settle into the trees. Brilliant shades of orange and pink flamed on the horizon and then gave way to gentle night tones of mauve and shady green as the sun sank lower. A soft breeze played over the hillside. The candles flickered and tiny tree frogs sang evening songs along the wooded banks of the creek.

Berry wiggled her bare toes in the grass. "This is better than beef Bourguignon. This is perfect." She studied Jake and secretly concluded he was the most perfect of all. His feet were bare, his long legs encased in clean faded jeans. A blue denim shirt casually draped over delicious broad shoulders. His eyes seemed smoky in the half light, hiding his thoughts.

Berry hoped her thoughts were just as well hidden. They were a confusing, painful mixture of hope and despair, love and anger, guilt and pride. Last Sunday she'd been so overwhelmed with love that she'd wanted to merge forever, body and soul, with Jake Sawyer. That had been wrong. You can't give up your identity and your goals in the name of love, she thought. It placed too heavy a burden on the other person. Successful relationships found a balance. That was the hard part, finding the balance.

The little dog curled up on a corner of the tablecloth and instantly fell asleep. Jake and Berry looked at the slumbering ball of fluff and exchanged smiles warm with parental puppy love. He covered her hand with his, and a ripple of excitement rushed through her stomach.

She'd always imagined a good marriage as being comfortable, and a good sexual relationship as being satisfying. Her relationship with Jake Sawyer had a few comfortable moments, but for the most part it was turmoil. And sex was not satisfying. It was exhausting, explosive, ecstatic, overwhelming. Life was hopelessly complicated, she decided. Just when she thought she had something figured out, it turned upside down.

She blinked in surprise when a raindrop

splashed on her nose. Another hit her forehead. "This has got to be the rainiest April ever," Berry said, helping Jake pack the dishes into the cardboard box. "I still haven't been able to open my apartment windows. The place smells worse than ever."

"I can't say I'm sorry. I like having you in my house." Jake rolled the puppy up in the tablecloth and handed her to Berry. "You take Calamity Jane."

They got to the house just as the rain turned heavy. Jake emptied the box on the kitchen counter and used the carton as a bed for the puppy. She half opened big brown eyes, made a muffled baby-dog sound, and went back to sleep.

Jake and Berry tiptoed from the kitchen to the living room, relit the candles, and made a fire in the Franklin stove. Jake plugged a dreamy CD into the stereo system. "Dance?"

Berry moved into the circle of his arms and relaxed against his body, noting how nicely they fit together. Memories of more intimate embraces flooded through her. They knew every square inch of each other. The slope of his hip was imprinted on her palm, the planes of his face embedded in her brain, his hard muscled thigh, the pulse point at the base of his neck. She knew every detail. It was nice to know another human being so thoroughly. It was special. Jake was special, and when she was in his arms like this her world was bliss. She cuddled closer and enjoyed the feel of his hands on her back.

The candle flames wavered in pools of molten wax, and the logs in the wood stove settled into glowing embers with a soft hiss. The stereo system automatically clicked off, but Jake continued to hold Berry in his arms.

Berry reluctantly raised her head from his shoulder and cocked an eyebrow as several car doors slammed in the distance, mingling with the muffled sounds of voices.

Jake looked down at Berry with the same puzzled expression. "Were you expecting company?"

The front door lock tumbled and Mrs. Fitz burst into the foyer, followed by Harry Fee, Miss Gaspich, Bill Kozinski, and a pack of senior citizens.

"You'll never guess!" Mrs. Fitz gestured at Berry

and Jake. "Mildred and Bill went and got married tonight! Isn't that wonderful?" She hugged Mildred and dabbed at her own red-rimmed eyes. "When they came in to the Pizza Place and told me, I called some friends from the Southside Hotel for Ladies. I thought we should have a party for them. You know, a wedding reception."

Berry's mouth went dry. Mildred Gaspich and Bill Kozinski married. How long had they known each other? Two weeks?

Jake's hand was at Berry's elbow, moving her forward. "That's wonderful. Congratulations." He steered Berry toward Mildred and Bill. "Berry and I are very happy for you."

"Berry don't look so happy," Mrs. Fitz said.

"She's surprised," Jake explained.

Berry managed a feeble smile. Pull yourself together! she ordered. You're supposed to be happy for them. She had a lump in her throat the size of a basketball, and blind panic raced helter-skelter through her brain. Mildred was married. How could she have acted so recklessly? Didn't she know the statistics on divorce? Why would she rush into a relationship that might fail?

Mrs. Fitz looked up at Jake. "Is it all right to

have a party? I guess I should have called first, but I got so excited."

Jake grinned. "Of course it's all right to have a party. It's not every day Mildred gets married to my sister's father-in-law." Jake turned to the flustered-looking bridegroom. "Have you called Penny and Frank?"

"Who?"

"Your son. His wife. My sister." Jake rolled his eyes. "Never mind, I'll call them."

An elderly woman with orange hair waved a brown paper sack in the air. "I brought my Sinatra collection. Where's the stereo?"

A case of beer appeared in the foyer. Two stout ladies staggered under a stack of steaming pizza boxes. "Where should we put these?"

Jake winced as the stereo blared Sinatra. "Good thing I don't have neighbors." He took Berry's hand and led her to the phone. "This hasn't exactly been the evening I'd planned."

"You're being a very good sport about it."

"I'm trying to impress you with my good-humored flexibility. I'm actually screaming inside. I was leading up to a grand finale." He dialed his sister's number and made no attempt to keep the laughter from his voice while he explained the occasion and invited them to the party. He turned back to Berry. "About my grand finale . . ."

Berry blew out a sigh. "I have to tell you, I was really looking forward to it."

Jake cracked his knuckles. "Me too. I was working myself up to it."

"You sound nervous."

"Scared to death. I've never done it before."

Never done it before? She thought they'd done everything. "This doesn't involve handcuffs, does it? Or leather stuff?"

Mrs. Fitz bustled past them. "We're out of ice cubes. Isn't this some party?"

"Yeah," Jake said, "some party. Wall-to-wall people. Where'd all these people come from? Do we know any of them?"

Berry self-consciously crossed her arms over her newfound cleavage. "Jake, about this grand finale. I'm sort of a traditional person."

"Damn, now I've made you nervous, too." His eyes traveled around the crowded house. "If only we could find some nice quiet place we could still do it."

"Well, ah . . . no sense being hasty about this. Maybe it would be best if we waited."

"Aha!" His face lit up. "The bathroom. We can do it in the bathroom."

Eek, Berry thought. What the heck was he going to do to her in the bathroom?

Jake draped his arm around her shoulders and pulled her into the powder room adjacent to the kitchen. He locked the door behind him and shoved his hands into his pockets. "Um, maybe you'd better sit down."

Berry looked at the only possible seat and cracked her knuckles. "Do I have to sit? I mean, couldn't we start out standing?"

"Sure. I just thought—this is a little awkward."

Awkward? This wasn't awkward. It was insane. The man had flipped. She must have flipped, too. Why else would she have followed him in here?

Jake looked thoughtful. "I'm not sure how to begin."

Oh, boy, this was going to be another disaster. She could feel it coming. Her mother had lived for fifty-two years without ever losing a mitten, much less a car. Her mother had a sane, orderly life that never included exploding cereal, burning apartments, or being locked in the bathroom with a crazy man. How did it happen that someone who'd inherited those sensible Scandinavian genes could be fated to stumble through life in such an absurd fashion?

"Listen, Jake, it isn't exactly that I have anything against doing it in the bathroom. After all, it was great in the shower, but this is different. This is sort of strange."

Jake grinned. "You think I brought you in here to ravish your body?"

"Of course not. That's ridiculous." She bit her lip. "Well, yes."

"Honey, that's so naughty."

Berry's cheeks flamed. "What the devil did you bring me in here for?"

"To propose."

She closed the lid and sat down with a thud. "Maybe I'll sit down after all."

Jake took a small blue velvet box from his pocket and assumed the traditional proposal position of kneeling on one knee. "Berry, will you . . ."

There was a knock at the door.

"Occupied!" Jake shouted. He popped the

ring box open, and a huge diamond twinkled at Berry. "I'd like to take more time with this, but someone wants to use the bathroom." He quickly slipped the ring on her limp finger. "Will you marry me?"

Berry sat absolutely mute, staring at the ring in dazed disbelief. What if she actually married him? Someday her children would ask how she got engaged, and she'd have to tell them it was while she was sitting on the toilet. Her mother got engaged at a church picnic. Her sister got engaged in a fancy restaurant. Lingonberry Knudsen got engaged on the toilet.

Jake patted her hand. "Too excited to speak?"

Berry opened her mouth, but no words emerged. Her mind was a blank. They hadn't invented words yet that suited this occasion.

"You feel okay? You're not going to faint, are you?"

Faint? Faint was the last thing she'd do. She was recovering from the shock, and she was damn mad. She was so mad her skin felt clammy and two bright red spots stained her cheeks. She clenched her fists and pressed her lips together.

Jake took a step backward. "Uh-oh, you're mad."

"Yes. No." She threw her hands into the air. "I don't know what I am!"

"I had a speech prepared, but some senior citizen has to use the facility."

This was a special moment for Jake, Berry realized. A fragile moment. And she didn't want to ruin it. She didn't want to rain on his parade. Problem was she had this anger. It was just there, bubbling inside her.

"I'm having issues," Berry said.

"Do you love me?"

"Of course I love you."

Jake wrapped his arms around her and kissed the top of her head. "Then everything will work out just fine."

There was another loud rap at the door.

Jake unlocked the door and ushered Berry past a wiry, gray-haired lady. "Sorry we took so long," he apologized.

"Merciful heavens," the woman exclaimed in a sharp intake of breath. She looked disapprovingly at Berry and slammed the door.

Mrs. Fitz suddenly appeared, shaking her

finger. "I saw the two of you come out of the bathroom together. What the devil were you doing in there?"

Jake held Berry's hand up to display the ring. "Getting engaged."

"That's wonderful!" Mrs. Fitz said, clasping her hands to her chest.

Berry snatched her hand away. "Actually, we were only talking about getting engaged. I don't think—"

"Listen up, everyone," Mrs. Fitz shouted. "Berry and Jake got engaged."

A pretty brunette extended her hand to Berry. "I'm Jake's sister Penny. I'm so relieved to see Jake's finally fallen in love. We thought it'd never happen." Penny grinned at her older brother. "Everyone in the family's tried to find a girl for Mr. Picky, here, but nothing doing. Jake always said he'd know when the right one came along, and he wasn't going to settle."

Jake slid his arm around Berry. "It's true. I said that."

Berry looked at the beautiful ring and felt her stomach turn. Was getting engaged supposed to make a person nauseous?

Chapter 9

Berry stood in the doorway and watched the last of Mildred's belongings get loaded into the back of the station wagon. She raised a hand and waved. "Good-bye," she whispered.

Jake put an arm around her. "Why so sad? Mildred and Bill will have a good life together."

Berry shrugged. She didn't know why she was sad, but she was dangerously close to crying. Mrs. Dugan was gone. Now Mildred was gone. Her newly adopted family was disbanding, and she felt bereft. "Guess I'm pretty silly, huh?"

"Yup." Jake held her close, resting his cheek against her curls.

"It isn't as if I'll never see them again. When Mildred and Bill come back from their honeymoon they'll be working at the Pizza Place just like always."

"Yup."

"And Mrs. Dugan will be home in another week."

"Yup."

"And I'm engaged," Berry added.

"You make it sound like a dental appointment."

Berry turned to face him. "I don't want you to take this personally, but being engaged upsets my stomach."

Jake looked down at her. "You don't want me to take that personally?"

"I didn't sleep a wink last night. I lay there all night long thinking about the dog, the house, the ring . . . you. It's like a dream come true. Everything I've always wanted has suddenly been dropped at my feet."

"So what's the problem?"

"Every time I look at this ring I get nauseous."

"Maybe you have the flu," Jake said.

"Maybe my stomach is smarter than my brain. Maybe it's trying to tell me something."

"Are you serious about this?"

"You think I'm crazy, huh?"

"The word *fruitcake* did flit through my mind."

Berry nervously twisted the ring on her finger. "But my stomach . . ."

"Don't listen to your stomach. Stomachs are stupid."

Berry's attention turned to the leggy kitten that strolled across the front lawn. "If it hadn't been for that cat we probably wouldn't be engaged."

Rrrrrf! Calamity Jane appeared in the doorway and raced down the lawn after the cat. The puppy stopped seven inches from the surprised kitten and bounced around. *Rrrrf. Rrrrrf.* The kitten narrowed its eyes and swiped at the dog's nose. Jane yelped and bolted for the house.

Just then Mrs. Fitz thundered down the stairs. "I see you," she said to Jane. "If I get hold of you there's gonna be dog stew." Mrs. Fitz waved a mangled piece of brown leather at Berry. "That blasted animal ate my pocketbook. It's a hazard to live here. Good thing I've got plans."

Berry raised her eyebrows. "Plans?"

Mrs. Fitz beamed. "Harry's on his way over here. He borrowed his son's motor home for a week, and we're gonna go see the Grand Canyon. I've never been there. I was worried about going away and leaving you alone at the Pizza Place, but Jake said it was okay. He said the two of you could handle it just fine."

"Jake knew about this?"

"Mrs. Fitz discussed it with me this morning while you were in the shower. I knew you wouldn't want to stand in the way of the Grand Canyon."

"Well, no, of course not, but what about the lunch contracts? I can't handle the lunch contracts alone, and you'll be teaching."

Jake opened the patio door to let some air into the house. "My teaching career has been cut short. Mrs. Newfarmer is feeling better, and she's returning to her class on Monday."

Berry jammed her fists onto her hips. "Nobody ever tells me anything. Why am I always the last to know what's going on around here?"

Mrs. Fitz pressed her lips together. "Because you either got your nose in a schoolbook or your hand in the refrigerator. And when you're not doing either of those, you're in the shower. Never seen anybody take so many showers. It's a wonder you haven't grown webbed feet."

"Showers relax me."

Jake looked at her sidewise.

"*Sometimes* they relax me."

A horn tooted outside, and Mrs. Fitz scrambled back upstairs. "That's Harry. Tell him I'll be right there. I'm just going to fetch my things."

Berry held tight to Jake's hand. "Mrs. Fitz is leaving! Do something."

"I offered to help with her luggage, but she said she was traveling light."

Berry grunted in exasperation. "I'm not talking about luggage. I'm talking about Mrs. Fitz and Harry. We have to stop them."

"Why?"

"Why? There are lots of good reasons."

"Uh-huh."

"They're old. What if they have a heart attack going through the desert? What if Mrs. Fitz forgets her blood pressure medicine? What if she can't find prune juice?"

"You sound like June Cleaver waiting for Wally to come home from his first date."

"Hell." She sat on the lowest step, resting her elbows on her knees, and her chin in her hands. Okay, Berry, she thought, what's the real *because*? Because I don't want to live all alone in this terrific house with Jake. Things were happening too fast. One minute she was delivering pizza to Quasimodo, and three weeks later she was engaged. Her stomach told her to take the ring off, but she couldn't—it was stuck. Stuck on her swollen finger, stuck to her love-struck heart. What a mess.

Mrs. Fitz sidled past her wearing jeans and a backpack. "What do you think?" she said, modeling her outfit. "Harry got these duds for me. Pretty nice, huh?"

Harry waved from the front door, and Mrs. Fitz hugged Berry. "Boy, this is gonna be great. Harry and I are gonna live in sin and see the Grand Canyon all at the same time. Isn't that something?"

Berry followed Mrs. Fitz to the front porch and watched the motor home rumble away. "When I grow up I want to be just like Mrs. Fitz."

There was the sound of glass breaking, followed by puppy feet clattering across the kitchen floor. Cat and dog burst out the front door and ran straight for Berry and Jake.

Jake snared Jane and carried her into the house. The cat held her ground on the porch, refusing to set foot inside.

"Smart cat," Berry said. "This house suddenly smells awful."

Jake's voice faltered. "I don't notice any smell."

"Are you kidding me? Any minute now the paint's going to start peeling off the walls. It smells like my apartment!"

"That's impossible."

"I'd know that stench anywhere. It reminds me of rotten fish in a gym locker."

Her face reflected total bafflement, and then the significance of the familiar odor began to register in her mind. She held a kitchen towel across her nose and headed for the basement.

"That smell is coming from your lab," Berry said.

Jake handed Jane over. "I'll go down and survey the damage."

Seconds later Jake rushed up the stairs and slammed the door behind him, gasping for air and grinning sheepishly. The expression on his flushed face was half embarrassed little boy and half unrepentant scoundrel.

"Looks like the animals chased each other around some down there and knocked over a few beakers. Nothing dangerous, but this house is going to smell like a dead groundhog for a few days. Even if I shut all the vents and doors, the fumes will still travel through the air-conditioning system."

The light bulb flicked on in Berry's head. That stinking odor had kept her from returning to her apartment. And it was manufactured in Jake Sawyer's cellar. "If there's one thing I can't stand," she said to him, "it's a sneaky chemist!"

"I prefer to think of myself as clever. I was a man on a mission."

Berry blew out a sigh. No one was ever going to accuse Jake Sawyer of being a quitter. And that was good, right? Tenacity was an admirable quality.

"Anyway, I only tricked you a little," Jake said. "In the beginning your apartment smelled bad all by itself."

"You've probably lied to me about all sorts of things. You've probably got a wife somewhere. Kids. More dogs."

Jake hadn't lied to her but he did have a secret, he thought. Eventually she'd find out, but not right now. He'd tell her when the time was right. After he was certain she loved him. The fact that she still had the ring on her finger was a good sign, right? It had to mean she was actually considering marrying him. He knew he was rushing her, but he had no choice.

Jake parked in front of the Pizza Place and reached behind him for Calamity Jane. He grabbed an armful of clothes from the backseat and waited patiently while the puppy wandered aimlessly around on the sidewalk.

"I'm not sure this is a good idea," Berry said. "My apartment is tiny, and I haven't had a chance to replace my furniture." And more to the point, there were no ladies to act as chaperones. They would be living together as if they were married, Berry thought. Her fear was that she would like it and she might be wearing a wedding band beside the engagement ring much sooner than she wanted. Act in haste, regret at leisure, her mother had always said.

"It will only be for a couple days," Jake told her. "As soon as my house gets back to normal we can move out of here."

Berry twisted the ring on her finger. She should have immediately taken it off, but she'd given in to circumstances. And now she was giving in to circumstances again. She wanted to believe she was being kind and sensitive, but she suspected she was just being a wimp. Not to mention there was a scary part of her that loved the ring and all it promised.

"Maybe she's empty," Jake said after a few minutes of no action from Jane.

He scooped the puppy up in his arms, and they all trooped upstairs. Berry opened windows that were still barren of curtains, and Jake set Jane down on the new carpet.

"Your apartment doesn't smell bad," Jake said. "The chemical is potent but not long-lived. It lasts two to three days at most, and I haven't been here since mid-week."

If and when there's a marriage, there will have to be clauses written into the vows, Berry thought. Thou shalt not give your wife experimental cereal, and thou shalt not brew and distribute stink oil without permission.

Jane was in the middle of the floor, sitting quietly.

"She has a strange expression on her face," Berry said.

Jake agreed. "She looks like she's concentrating."

And then without warning, Jane stood and burped and pooped on the new carpet.

Berry was speechless.

"Maybe we should have one of these rooms carpeted with grass," Jake said.

Ten minutes later the poop was bagged and carted outside to the trash, and the carpet had been cleaned to within an inch of its life. Jane was running in circles, and Berry was at the kitchen sink doing a surgical-quality scrub on her hands. She had soapsuds up to her elbows, and she was wondering if she was cut out for motherhood. The floppy-eared dogs and the kids sounded good on paper, but this was reality and her apartment was back to smelling stinky. She lathered herself one last time and the diamond ring slipped off her finger, sailed through the air, and bounced onto the carpet in front of Jane. In an instant the ring was nowhere to be seen.

Berry's eyes opened wide. "I think Jane just ate the ring."

Jake looked skeptically at the little dog. "That's impossible."

"Honest to goodness, I think she swallowed the ring."

Jake dropped to his knees and raked his hand through the carpet. "Jane, you canine garbage pail, tell me you didn't eat that expensive, undigestible ring."

"Oh, Lord, what's going to happen to her?" Berry carefully cradled the fat puppy. "Will she be all right? Will she die? Dogs can't eat rings, can they?"

"To begin with, we're not even sure if she ate the ring."

They crawled around on the rug for several minutes, searching in vain for the diamond.

Berry had difficulty finding her voice. "It's not here. Maybe we should take her to a vet."

Jake stroked a soft, floppy ear. "I suppose we should."

Berry held the dog close and headed for the stairs. "There's a veterinary clinic just a couple blocks from here. I pass it on my way to school. I think it's one of those twenty-four-hour emergency things so maybe it will be open on Sunday."

Jake drove, and Berry held Jane while she whimpered and wriggled.

"It's okay, Jane," Berry said. "We're almost there. The vet will know what to do."

Jake opened the clinic door to an empty well-lit waiting room. "Guess there's not much happening in the veterinary world on Sunday morning."

The receptionist glanced up from her computer and smiled. "We don't schedule appointments on Sunday. Only emergency cases. Is this an emergency?"

"We think the puppy ate a ring. A big expensive ring."

The receptionist nodded sympathetically. "That could be an emergency." She gave Jake a card to fill out. "I'll get Dr. Pruett."

"I hope Dr. Pruett knows what he's doing," Berry whispered to Jake. "Maybe we should have taken Jane to a specialist."

"Maybe we should have taken her to a jeweler." Jake slid an arm around Berry's shoulders. "Honey, she's going to be fine."

"I know."

"Then why is that tear hanging onto your eyelashes?"

"Poor Jane. She's just a baby, and she has a scratchy ring inside her."

Jake cradled Berry in his arms, being careful

not to squash the panting puppy. "You love her, huh?"

Berry sobbed a strangled "Yes," and buried her face in his shoulder. "Why does love always have to be so painful?"

"It's not always painful." He tenderly kissed her temple. "Jane probably thinks love is pretty great. She's so happy to be getting all this attention and affection, she probably doesn't even notice the ring in her stomach."

Berry let her cheek rest against his chest. "You think so?" It was a nice thought, that she could make Jane feel better just by loving her.

The receptionist beckoned from the hallway. "Mr. and Mrs. Sawyer, you can take Jane into Examining Room Two. Dr. Pruett will be right with you."

Berry opened her mouth to correct the receptionist and then thought better of it. It was an innocent enough misunderstanding, and it was sort of fun to test-drive the name. Mrs. Sawyer. Mrs. *Berry* Sawyer. It had a certain sound to it. Besides, she reasoned, it legitimized their puppy.

Dr. Pruett was a short, stocky man with a receding hairline and an obvious love of animals. He scratched Jane's neck while he took her temperature and told her dog jokes when he examined her teeth. "She seems to be in perfect health," he told Jake and Berry. "With the exception of possibly having a diamond stuck somewhere in her gizzards." He tucked Jane under his arm. "I'm going to take a couple X-rays. We'll be right back."

"X-rays," Berry worried, "that sounds so serious. And do you suppose they're safe? She's just a baby."

Ten minutes later Dr. Pruett returned with Jane and proudly displayed her X-rays. "There it is! She swallowed the ring, all right. It's lodged in her stomach." He turned to Jake. "Looks to me like you're engaged to a cocker spaniel."

Berry gripped Jake's hand. "Does she have to be operated on?"

Dr. Pruett stroked the glossy black ears. "There's a good chance that she'll pass the ring all by herself. If you like, you can leave Jane here for a day or two. We'll keep a real close watch on her and feed her a little mineral oil to help ease things along."

Berry nodded numbly. "You'll call us if anything happens?"

"For sure," Dr. Pruett said. "You'll be the second to know."

Whump. Berry slammed the wad of pizza dough onto the butcher-block table and punched it with her fist.

Jake watched out of the corner of his eye and flinched. "You're not very big, but you sure do pack a wallop."

Thwup. Berry hit it with the rolling pin. "I get rid of my frustrations this way."

"You must be really frustrated. You've been beating up on that dough all day." He leaned across the table at her. "You want to know how I get rid of my frustrations?"

"No!"

"Are these frustrations of yours physical in nature?" he asked.

"No."

His voice gentled. "Want to talk about it?"

Berry sighed and pushed her curls behind her ears, leaving white flour smudges on her flushed cheeks. "No."

What was there to talk about? She was confused and scared. Her heart told her to marry Jake, and her head told her not to rush into anything.

Jake slouched against the counter. "I hate to ruin your fun, but it's ten o'clock. We've had three customers in the past two hours, and you've got enough pizza crusts to last through November. What do you say we call it a night?"

Berry looked up from her pounding. "It's ten o'clock already?"

His silky voice held a teasing challenge. "If I didn't know better, I'd guess you were avoiding going to bed with me."

Berry dusted her hands off on her apron and tipped her nose defiantly into the air. "That's absurd. And I'm not going to bed with you. We're going to bed separately. I go into my bedroom, shut my door, and go to sleep. You sleep . . . somewhere else."

"Where else am I supposed to sleep? You don't even have a couch. And besides, we're engaged, we're adults, and we're in love. Am I right?"

Berry nodded. All that was true.

"Here's the problem," she said to Jake. "We're two entirely different kinds of people. You're a risk taker. You're a man who trusts his instincts. I'm more of a plodder. Look at my shoes." Berry stared down at her feet. "I wear running shoes. A trustworthy brand. Not too cheap, not too expensive. Middle-of-the-road shoes. I've worn middle-of-the-road shoes all my life, and I've never been really sure where they were taking me until a year ago when I went back to school and bought the Pizza Place. It was really difficult to scrape the money together. I had to talk a bank into taking a chance on me. I had no collateral and no business experience, but I had confidence that I could succeed. Now, thanks to the lunch contracts, my pizza business is in the black. I made a sound business decision, I stuck by it, and I succeeded."

"And?"

"And while that felt like the logical, sensible thing to do . . . marriage right now feels impetuous."

"Okay," Jake said. "I can appreciate your point of view. Let's temporarily take marriage out of the equation and just get to know each other."

"Does that involve sleeping together?'

"Yes."

"Without the imminent threat of marriage?"

"Yes." At least for tonight, Jake thought.

Chapter 10

Berry opened one eye and sniffed. Someone was cooking bacon. She snatched at the digital clock on her nightstand and squinted at it. Someone was cooking bacon at *five o'clock in the morning*. She ran her hand through her tangled hair, wrapped a short terry robe over her University of Washington nightshirt, and shuffled out to the kitchen.

Jake waved a spatula at her in greeting.

"What on earth are you doing?" Berry asked.

"Making us breakfast. I knew the smell of bacon would get you stumbling out here."

"It's five in the morning. Couldn't you get me stumbling out at seven or eight?"

"Have you forgotten what day this is? This is not an ordinary day."

Jake poured Berry a cup of coffee and set a plate of scrambled eggs, a buttered muffin, and half a pound of bacon in front of her.

"Isn't this the day you take your art history exam?" he asked. "I know you've been studying for it all week, and then you had sort of a disruptive weekend. So I thought you'd probably want to get up early and do some last-minute cramming." He plunked her school notebook beside her plate.

There you have it, Berry thought. Good sex makes you stupid. All the blood rushes from your brain to other body parts and there's nothing left in your head but euphoria. And whatever the price, the experience was worth it. Sleeping with Jake Sawyer was a life-changing experience. It was *wow*. It was *yummmm*. It was *yes*! And as if this orgasmic miracle wasn't enough, the man had gotten up early to make her breakfast.

Suddenly there was a mental thunderclap and bolt of lightning, and Berry figured it out. They were a team. A *good* team. If they just worked together, there wasn't anything they couldn't do. They could sell pizza, invent glop, raise puppies, and love each other. Berry didn't have to do it all alone.

Jake cocked an eyebrow at her. "You have the strangest expression on your face. Are you feeling okay?"

"I'm feeling wonderful. I'm going to eat this entire scrumptious breakfast, then I'm going to study my brains out until two o'clock, and when I come back from my exam I have big plans."

Jake sat opposite her and forked into his eggs. "When you come back from your exam, if I'm not mistaken, you're going to have to study economics."

At ten o'clock in the morning the phone rang.

"It's Dr. Pruett," Jake called to Berry. "Good news. The ring is in Jane's intestines. Not long now!"

Berry smiled. Everything in her life was turning out right. She'd probably ace her art history exam. She didn't know why she was bothering to study. "You sound like an expectant father, waiting for your spaniel to deliver a healthy one-carat ring."

Jake shook his head in amazement. "Two months ago if anyone had told me I'd be this worried over a dog, I'd have told them they were crazy."

"She'll be fine."

His eyes watched her intently. "Something strange is going on here. That was my line last night. Now you're reassuring *me*."

"That's because I feel fine." She shook her pencil at him for emphasis. "Not everyone can be a successful pizza tycoon."

"That's what's important to you, huh? Being a pizza tycoon?"

Berry buried her nose in her art book. "Nope. I don't give a fig about pizza. It's the success part."

Jake stared at her for a moment, lost in thought. He nodded slightly, as if he understood, and kissed her lightly on the top of her head. "I don't give a fig about pizza, either. Nevertheless, I shall now descend to the bowels of the Pizza Place and work my fingers to the bone fulfilling lunch contracts. Do you know why I'm going to do this?"

"I can hardly wait to hear."

"I got rid of your ladies for the express purpose of getting you into the sack, and now that I've boinked the pizza tycoon I have to pay the piper."

Berry gave the door to the Pizza Place a shove and staggered to the counter where Jake was working. "One more slide of sixteenth-century bucolic splendor, and my eyes will fall out of my head."

Jake wiped his hands on his apron. "Tough exam?"

"I don't know. My mind is numb."

"Good thing you only have one more exam."

"Yeah, good thing." Her attention was diverted by a yelp from the corner of the small restaurant area. "Jane!"

The little black dog was confined in a playpen. She hopped up and down at the sight of Berry. She wagged her tail and made excited puppy sounds and rolled on the plastic playpen mat.

Berry rushed over and hugged Jane. "She remembers me. She's so smart!"

"Not only is she smart, but she's also empty, if you know what I mean."

"What a good dog." Berry laid her cheek against the silky black head. "It was so clever of you to get rid of that ring."

Jake delivered a salad and a hamburger to the table nearest the playpen. "Come here, Goldilocks. I made you some supper, and then you're excused to go upstairs and study."

"Yum, I'm famished." She plopped the puppy back into the playpen.

"No more upset stomachs?"

"Nope. All gone. I'm fine. Never been better in my whole life."

Jake stiffened. "Great. I suppose that makes you real happy."

"Yup." She munched on a carrot stick and watched Jane attack a rope dog bone.

He gave it his best shot, Jake thought, but in the end she had to get rid of the ring to feel good. And he was almost out of time. He was hopelessly in love and he was running out of time.

"This playpen is a great idea," Berry said.

"I borrowed it from my sister. She's one of those family-type people."

Now what? Berry wondered. All of a sudden

he sounds absolutely cranky. She ate the last bite of hamburger and stabbed a lone chunk of raw broccoli from her salad bowl. "Well, that was terrific. Guess I'll go hit the books now."

Jake bent over a wad of pizza dough. *Whump.* He smacked it with the rolling pin.

Wow, Berry thought, I've never seen him whack pizza dough around like that. Maybe he's cracking under the strain of fatherhood. Maybe he isn't ready to have puppies. Boy, wouldn't that be the pits? Here I am all set to go off and start researching baby food, and Jake gets cold feet. Well, if that's the problem, we'll work it out together. We're a team. She smiled at a scowling Jake and hummed as she went through the door.

Several hours later Berry was startled out of her studying by stomping and thumping on the stairs. Jake swung the collapsed playpen around the corner and unceremoniously tumbled a squirming puppy onto the rug. "Damn, I didn't think I was going to make it. This dog didn't want to hold still."

Berry closed her economics book and stood at her seat by the table. He was still cranky. Can't blame him, she decided. He's had a long day. Up at five to help me study. Worked making pizza for twelve hours. And somewhere in between he's had to be responsible for Jane.

Rrrrf, Jane squeaked, running in circles, chasing her tail.

Well, all that was about to end, Berry thought. He could relax now. She'd take care of Jane. She'd show him they could be a team and raise puppies by the hundreds. She grabbed Jane and kissed the top of her head. "Has the puppy eaten?"

"She had a pepperoni pizza at about seven."

"Is she allowed to eat that? I mean isn't she on a special diet after her ordeal?"

Jake gave her a black look. "I let her run around loose as a special treat, and she ate some guy's pizza when he went to the john."

"Oh, dear."

"She even ate his napkin."

"Anything else I should know about? How's her stomach?"

"Her stomach's fine. How's *your* stomach?"

Obviously he didn't want to talk about the dog. "My stomach's okay."

"Humph." He slouched onto a kitchen chair and turned his attention to the newspaper.

Humph? What kind of an answer was *humph?* How was she supposed to make conversation with a man that said *humph* and then pressed his nose into the sports page? She had to tell him about success and failure and commitment. She was ready for all that stuff. More than ready—practically panting. Marriage would be wonderful this time. She looked at Jake and thought her heart would burst. Lord, she loved him. Allen had been a roommate. Jake was her friend, her lover, her helpmate, her hero. She hugged herself and twirled around as she went to the kitchen to fill a water bowl for the puppy.

Jake squinted at her antics over the top of his paper. "Humph," he mumbled, rattling the funnies.

Berry glared down at him. "What's all this *humph?*"

"It's nothing," he said. "I'm just happy to see you so happy."

"Do you know what would make me *really* happy? Going to bed. Are you coming with me?"

Jake stayed hidden behind his paper.

"Okay," Berry said. "I'm going to take that as a yes. I'm going to take a nice long, soapy shower and then I'm going to take my overheated naked body to bed."

Thirty minutes later, Berry was in bed alone and her overheated naked body was cooling off fast. Now what? Where the heck was he? She rolled out of bed and stomped out to the darkened living room.

When her eyes adjusted to the dim light, she blinked in disbelief at the inert form stretched out on the floor. Jake was asleep! Berry stood openmouthed, listening to his gentle regular breathing, watching the slow rise and fall of his chest. The puppy slept beside him, curled into a ball, tucked securely under his left armpit. Adorable, she thought. And all done in. Obviously they'd both had an exhausting day. She tucked a quilt around them and went to bed. She shut off the lamp on her nightstand. She watched the minutes change on her digital clock. She watched the lights of passing cars reflect on her window shade. She picked the nail polish off her index finger.

"I can't sleep," she groaned. "I'm in lust."

Okay, we'll do this scientifically. Relax toes. Relax ankles. Relax knees. Relax thighs. Relax whatever was next. It wasn't working! She turned onto her stomach and smushed her face into the pillow. She needed something to get her mind off her body. She could worry about Mrs. Dugan. Mrs. Fitz and Harry were wheeling their way south. Berry opened one eye and checked out the clock. What was Mrs. Fitz doing right now? Berry rolled her eyes. They were probably in bed. Together! Damn. She flung herself onto her back and thrashed around until she was hopelessly tangled in the sheet. This was all Jake's fault, the slimeball. How dare he sleep when she was in such a state.

She heard rustling in the living room, and a band of light flashed on under her door.

"What the devil?" Jake mumbled. "Oh, damn!"

Berry thought about it for a minute and reached the obvious conclusion. "Pepperoni pizza?" she called to Jake.

"My dream about a floppy-eared dog didn't include this."

"Is Jane okay?"

"Jane is great. I put her in the playpen, and she's asleep already."

Berry hugged herself and curled her toes. What a shame. Now Jake was going to have to take a shower and find another place to sleep. She smoothed the sheets and plumped her pillow.

Jake stormed into the bathroom, muttering colorful phrases, and slammed the door. Minutes later he emerged with damp hair and a towel precariously draped on his hips. He stood at the edge of the bed and peered at Berry in the semidarkness. "Well?"

Berry looked up at him. "Well what?"

Jake dropped his towel and slid under the quilt and turned to Berry. "Listen, Berry—" He sighed heavily and rolled away from her. "Oh, hell."

Something was going wrong here, Berry thought. She was in bed with a naked man, and he just turned his back on her. She understood about being tired, but this was going too far. This was getting insulting. So, the hell with him. She rolled away and straightened the sheet. She shaped her pillow just so. She looked for just the perfect position.

"Berry."

"You growled?"

"What are you doing? Practicing the polka?"

"I can't get comfortable."

"It would be nice if you didn't make it *my* problem. I've had a lousy day. I'd like nothing better than to get back to sleep."

"Ugh." Berry smacked him with her pillow.

Jake snatched the pillow from her and tucked it under his head.

"Jake Sawyer, give me back my pillow!"

"Possession is nine-tenths of the law. It's mine now."

Berry ripped the quilt from him and wrapped herself in it cocoon style, gloating over the gasp of surprise she'd provoked. Two could play this game. He wasn't the only one who was capable of acting childish.

Jake grabbed an end and dumped her out of the quilt.

"Hey, possession is nine-tenths of the law!" Berry said.

"Only when you're big and strong like me." He placed the pillow in the middle of the bed and pointed with his finger. "That half of the pillow is yours." He draped the quilt over them and tucked her in. "How's your stomach?"

"It's fine. How's yours?"

What was with this stomach stuff? That had to be the third time tonight he'd asked about her stomach.

"Mmmph." He slammed his head onto his half of the pillow.

"We don't fit like this," Berry said. "I can't get my head onto my half of the pillow."

He silently rolled to his side, and Berry inched her way over. Now they were back to back, tush to tush. Berry watched the digital minutes tick by. She couldn't sleep like this. Tush to tush was uncomfortable. She held her breath and very carefully rolled over until she was facing Jake, spoon fashion. Yes, she decided, this was much better.

For lack of something better to do with her arm, she draped it over his waist and rested her cheek just millimeters from his neck. Mmmm, she was getting more comfortable all the time, but the angle was wrong. She was sure she could go to sleep if she was just a bit closer, so she wriggled around until she was perfectly molded to Jake's back. She finally had attained the ideal position for sleep, and she was so pleased about it that she allowed herself a sigh of satisfaction. "Ahhh," she sighed softly, blowing a little wisp of warm air across his neck, into his ear.

"Ohhh!"

"Pardon?" she whispered, her voice husky with thoughts of sleep.

Jake's voice cracked when he spoke. "Are you comfortable?"

Berry stretched slightly, pressing her breasts into his back. "Mmmm. Are you?"

There was a low groan, and she felt his muscles tense.

"I'm so tired," she said. "I can hardly keep my eyes open. How about you?"

"I'm not tired at all. To tell you the truth, I'm wide-awake. In fact, I'm getting more awake by the minute."

Berry's finger carelessly stroked the center of Jake's belly. "Maybe, you just need some relaxing."

"Relax? With your breasts poking into my back and your finger stuck in my navel?" He gave a sigh of desperation and turned around to face her. "Listen, Berry, there's something I have to tell you."

Berry felt his arousal hard and full against her, cleverly sneaking its way under her night-shirt. She ran her hands across his smooth muscular back and kissed the pulse point that throbbed in his neck. She loved him. With all her heart and soul and every hormone she possessed. She loved the way he got excited about his crazy food inventions, and the way he accepted the ladies. He could bandage a scratch, inflate a sagging ego, make a helluva pepperoni pizza, and turn her into mush with a single glance.

"I have a few things to tell you, too," Berry said. "The first thing I need to tell you is that I'm going to make mad, passionate love to you."

Chapter 11

Berry thought she might begin to purr. It was a wonderful luxury to awaken in the arms of your lover. Especially when your lover was about to become your husband and the father of your children. At least she assumed he was about to become her husband and the father of the children. Actually, he hadn't mentioned marriage last night. And now that she thought about it, he hadn't returned the ring. She pressed her cheek to his chest and listened to the steady beat of his heart while he slept. Good thing she was secure and not the sort to panic. If she was the sort to panic, she might worry that he'd caught cold feet from her.

There was a squeal of brakes on the street and the angry slam of a car door. "And another thing," a familiar voice shouted. "I don't snore. *You* snore!"

Mrs. Fitz? Berry rolled out of bed and went to the window.

Mrs. Fitz looked up at her. "What the devil are you doing here? Why aren't you at the house?"

"It's a long story," Berry said. "Why aren't you on your way to the Grand Canyon?"

Mrs. Fitz flapped her arms at the departing camper. "You ever try to live in one of them things with an old man? It was enough to take seven years off my life. He drives like a maniac. He makes disgusting slurping noises at breakfast. And I can't stand the way he blows his nose. He honks. You don't have to honk when you blow your nose." She fished in her purse and inserted her key in the door. "Boy, it's good to be home. I can't wait to make myself a cup of tea."

"I just had the scariest dream," Jake said, sitting up in bed. "I thought I heard Mrs. Fitz saying it was good to be home."

Berry slumped against the wall. "That was no dream. Harry slurped and honked, so Mrs. Fitz dumped him." She pulled on a pair of jeans and dropped a yellow T-shirt over her head. "I'll make coffee and you can take Jane for a walk."

"Old men," Mrs. Fitz muttered in the kitchen. "Don't ever go camping with an old man. Nothing but a pain in the behind."

"I thought you and Harry got along so well."

"Yeah, well, you never really know a man until you've had to sit across from him at the breakfast table."

Berry leaned against the counter while the coffee dripped. "Jake is sensational at the breakfast table."

"Yeah. After you've eaten breakfast with Jake, you're ruined," Mrs. Fitz said.

Voices carried up to them from the street. Berry and Mrs. Fitz looked at each other and raised their eyebrows when the downstairs door opened.

"Better not be Harry coming back. I'm done with him," Mrs. Fitz said, angrily folding her arms across her chest.

Berry leaned forward. "It's not Harry. It's Mildred and Bill—and Mrs. Dugan!"

"I got food poisoning," Mrs. Dugan said when she walked into the apartment. "Thought I was going to die. The ship company was real nice about it. They put me up in a hospital in Vancouver for two days and then flew me home. I tried calling last night from the airport, but there wasn't any answer at the house, and the Pizza Place line was always busy."

"So she called me," Mildred said. "Lucky we came home from our honeymoon early." She nudged Mrs. Dugan in the arm. "Tell them about Stanley."

Mrs. Dugan poured herself a cup of tea. "Before I got sick I met the nicest man. He lives just blocks from here. Can you imagine that?"

"Has he got friends?" Mrs. Fitz asked. "I need a new boyfriend."

Bill helped himself to an English muffin. "Nicky Petrowski's going to be glad to hear that. He saw you at our party and thought you were really something."

Mrs. Fitz looked skeptical. "Nicky Petrowski. Was he the one with the tattoo on his forehead?"

"Naw, that's Bucky Weaver. He's missing a few marbles. I don't think you want to go out with Bucky Weaver. Nicky Petrowski's the one who can touch his nose with his tongue."

"I remember him. He's real cute," Mrs. Fitz said.

Berry glanced at the clock and drained her coffee cup. "I'd like to stay and hear more about Nicky Petrowski's talents, but I've got to take an economics exam this morning."

"I'll drop you off at school," Jake said, taking a set of keys from the kitchen counter.

The drive to the college was quiet. Berry stared at her naked ring finger and wondered if she was still engaged. She was afraid to ask. What if he said no? She tilted her chin up a fraction of an inch. Then she'd make the best of it. Obviously, he enjoyed sleeping with her. If that was to be the extent of their relationship, she'd just have to go day by day and try to put limitations on her feelings.

Lord, how did you do that when you were coconuts over someone? Maybe in time, she decided. Maybe after a while his feelings would turn back to marriage. She clasped her hands together. It was going to hurt to have to wait. She wanted to be a permanent part of him now. There were things she had to share with him . . . silly jokes, comfortable silences, promotions, rejections, income tax audits, childbirth. Especially childbirth. She pressed her lips together and stole a brief glance at Jake. Ironic that she finally understood his impatience, just when he seemed to have adopted her reluctance.

Jake pulled to the curb and let the engine idle. A muscle worked in his jaw while he stared at the steering wheel.

Berry's stomach turned. This is it, she thought, barely able to breathe. He's going to dump me. This is the kiss-off. Good-bye, Berry, it's been fun.

"Berry, there's something I have to tell you."

She was going to be sick. Or she was going to cry. Maybe she'd do both. Shape up, Berry, she ordered. You can't throw up in this car. It's a rental.

"You're as white as a sheet! Is it your stomach?" Jake asked hopefully, putting his hand to her forehead.

He sounded happy. Probably he'd go into ecstasy if she had dysentery. "It's my exam. I'm worried about my exam."

"Maybe we should talk later."

"Yeah, later would be better."

Berry skipped down the classroom building steps in a state of giddy relief. It was over, and she knew she'd passed both her exams with flying colors. If she took courses this summer, she'd be a senior in the fall.

A long arm reached out and snagged her by the elbow. "Whoa, where's the rush?"

Berry looked around and realized it was Jake.

"I'm done," Berry said. "I passed. I know this sounds silly, but I felt like I needed to run."

The somber mood was instantly replaced with a smile that only partially reached his eyes. "That's great. I'm happy for you."

Berry clutched her books to her chest. "I suppose we have to talk now."

"I suppose we do." He plunged his hands into his pockets and studied his shoes. "I have some good news, and some bad news." He looked around. "Would you mind if we went back to the house where it's more private?"

She nodded and followed him to the car. It didn't take a genius to see his mood wasn't good. Well, phooey, so what if he gives me the old heave-ho. There are lots more where he came from. She shook her head. Berry, Berry, Berry. Who are you trying to kid? Like Mrs. Fitz said, after you've eaten breakfast with Jake Sawyer, you're ruined.

"Where's the station wagon?" Berry asked, shading her eyes from the sun, looking for the car.

"That's part of the good news. I bought a new car. What do you think?"

"This is your new car? This flashy red number? Wow, what is it?"

"It's a Ferrari."

Holy cow, a Ferrari. It looked like it should come equipped with James Bond. Berry slid into the passenger seat. Major depression. This was *not* a family car. He probably bought the darn thing with the money he got back from the ring. "Okay, let's go. Let's get to the house so I can hear the bad news. Boy, I can't wait. I love bad news."

Jake crept out into the afternoon traffic. "It's not such bad news. Good news and bad news is a figure of speech. Actually, the bad news is sort of boring. It's not worth getting upset over. Maybe it's the car that's upsetting you. Do you hate the car?"

"Are you kidding? How could anyone hate this car? This car is nifty."

Of course I hate the car, you insensitive bachelor, she thought. Why couldn't you buy a four-door sedan? You could put a pregnant wife and kids in a four-door sedan. Or better yet, station wagon. Then the dogs would fit. She folded her arms across her chest and slunk down in her seat. Tomorrow she would cry her eyes out and smash pizza dough until she was exhausted. It's not so bad, she told herself. You've been through this before. You know how to repair a broken heart and damaged ego.

Jake parked in the driveway and fiddled with his keys. He looked at the house and sighed. "The bad news is . . . the house still smells."

"That's the bad news?" Berry didn't know whether to scream, cry, or burst out laughing. Get a grip, she told herself. You're getting hysterical.

"I know you're really ticked off about this smell business. It's just that I was in such a panic. I was so crazy in love with you that I couldn't think straight. All I knew was that I couldn't live without you. You made this big, empty house into a home. The minute you stepped through the door I could smell pudding cooking on the stove and hear kids running up and down the stairs. That was when I made up my plan. All I could think about, day and night, was having you by my side and buying a dog. I know it was dumb of me to rush out and buy Jane, but it symbolized commitment to me. I guess it was a way of reassuring myself that everything would work out and that you would be a permanent part of my life." He thumped the steering wheel. "Man, I really screwed this up. I just thought, maybe if you had longer to get to know me you could learn to like me. Honey, I love you more than life itself. I know it makes you sick to your stomach to wear my ring, but I'm willing to wait. We could live together for a while. No pressure until you're ready. I promise I won't mention the ring again. We don't even have to have kids right away. We could get another dog." He saw the look of horror on her face and held up his hands. "Okay, no more dogs."

"Is this why you kept asking me about my stomach?"

"As soon as you got the ring off your finger, your stomach felt fine. Boy, talk about depressing."

Berry gave her head a small shake. "We've got to work on communication. My stomach felt fine because I realized I loved you and we were a really good team."

"I didn't know," Jake said. "You didn't tell me."

"I guess I have a lot of explaining to do," Berry said, "but first, I think I'm going to make love with you in this flashy car."

"It's not very big."

"It will be when I'm done with it."

Jake's eyes crinkled into laugh lines. "I meant the car."

"Of course. I knew that. Are you going to argue with me about this, or what?"

"I think I'm going to *or what*."

Half an hour later they rolled out of the

car onto the grass and lay there sweating and laughing.

"Well, we did it," Berry gasped, straightening her shirt.

"My back will never be the same. I think I'm too old for this car stuff." He looked over at her. "Tonight I'm going to do it right—soft music, candles, nice sheets."

"Sounds wonderful, but we have wall-to-wall ladies in my apartment."

"I never told you the rest of the good news. I've sold partial rights to a computer game I originally designed for my nephew. And next month United Foods will begin introducing an entire line of Jake's Junk. We're moderately rich. We can sleep wherever we want tonight. Juneau, Japan, the Grand Canyon." His eyes held hers in a silent affirmation of love. "I want to make things nice for you. If you want to finish school and be a pizza tycoon, that's fine. But I want to pamper you a little, too."

Berry lazily watched Jake reach into his jeans pocket and extract something that flashed in the waning sunlight.

"My ring!" Berry exclaimed.

"I've had it sterilized and sized." He slipped the ring on her finger. "This is just as binding as a marriage ceremony, Lingonberry Knudsen. I promise to love you forever and ever, good times, bad times, till death do us part."

"Till death do us part," she repeated. "Good times, bad times, love everlasting."

"There's just one more thing," Jake said. "Now that you've pledged good times and bad times and love everlasting I have a confession to make."

"Already?"

"I've been saving it for the right moment."

"And the right moment would be what?"

"It would be after you pledged to stick with me through bad times."

"Oh, boy."

"My aunt Bitsy is coming to visit tomorrow," Jake said. "She's my grandmother's sister, and she makes Mrs. Dugan look like loosey-goosey. Don't get me wrong, she's a nice lady. It's just that her moral code is left over from Victorian England, and honestly she's always scared the bejeezus out of me."

"How long is she staying?"

"A week! An entire week. Seven days. A hundred and sixty-eight hours. She'll inspect glasses for water spots. She'll make me polish my shoes and eat all my vegetables. And there'll be no hanky-panky. I was really hoping I could get you to marry me before she arrived, but at least you've pledged bad times."

"It's just a week," Berry said.

"Trust me, it'll be a *long* week."

Berry didn't think it sounded so bad. She was going to have another little old lady to chat with at the breakfast table. And Berry thought if she could hurry Jake along, they could be married before Aunt Bitsy arrived.

Enter the World of Janet Evanovich

Don't miss any of her early romances!

The Rocky Road to Romance

Her tall, dark, and deliciously dangerous boss . . .

When the delightful, daffy Dog Lady
of station WZZZ offered to take on the
temporary job of traffic reporter, Steve
Crow tried to think of reasons to turn
Daisy Adams down. Perhaps he knew
that sharing the close quarters of a
car with her for hours would give the
handsome program director no room to
resist her quirky charms. He'd always
favored low-slung sports cars and high-
heeled women, but that was before he
fell for a free spirit who caught crooks
by accident, loved old people and pets,
and had just too many jobs!

Loving Daisy turned Steve's life upside
down, especially once he adopted Bob,
a huge dog masquerading as a couch
potato. But was Daisy finally ready to
play for keeps?

Love Overboard

Sinfully handsome schooner captain Ivan Rasmussen deserved to be called Ivan the Terrible, Stephanie Lowe decided. First he'd sold her a haunted house, and now he was laughing at her Calamity Jane cooking! She'd only agreed to work one voyage of his Maine coastal cruise in exchange for the house repairs promised by her cousin, who'd run off to marry a plumber.

But the brazen Ivan, descendant of a pirate, insisted on flirting with her. When the voyage ended, he even managed to be on hand to help her trap the "ghost" in her house. Fun and comic mayhem, as only Janet Evanovich can write it.

Back to the Bedroom

For months he'd thought of her as the Mystery Woman, draped in black velvet cloak, with outrageous red curls, flawless skin, and carrying a large, odd case. But the night David Dodd sees a helicopter drop a chunk of metal through the roof of his lovely neighbor's bedroom, he gets to meet the formidable and delightful Katherine Finn at last!

Kate is a driven concert musician with more commitments than hours in the day. Dave is a likable slacker who seems to be drifting through life. Yet, no one has ever made her feel as cherished, and she's never had so much fun, but even though, her eccentric boarder, Elise, assures her that where Kate is concerned Dave has plenty of ambition.

Manhunt

Alexandra Scott, Alaskan Wilderness Woman. It had a terrific ring to it, but Alex felt a sudden twinge of uncertainty. She'd traded in her Wall Street job and fancy condo for a rundown cabin in the woods and a bait & tackle store. She'd wanted to escape the rat race and to go husband-hunting where men outnumbered women four to one, but was she ready for the challenge?

Then she spotted Michael Casey, a sexy pilot who was undaunted by disaster, had hero written all over him . . . and was a confirmed bachelor. Michael Casey was the man she had come to Alaska to hunt, and Alexandra Scott had him in her sights.

Smitten

Single mom Lizabeth Kane wasn't exactly construction-worker material, but she truly wanted a job—and Matt Hallahan found her radiant smile utterly irresistible. When he agreed to hire her as a laborer, Lizabeth sent up a cheer. Since her divorce from a snobby philanderer, she'd frankly lost interest in men, but this macho carpenter who smelled of sawdust and musk made her senses sizzle.

As for Matt, he was charmed by Lizabeth's enthusiasm, her spunky kids and wacky aunt. Clearly this was a match made in heaven.

Thanksgiving

When Megan Murphy discovers a floppy-eared rabbit gnawing on the hem of her skirt, she means to give its careless owner a piece of her mind— but Dr. Patrick Hunter is too attractive to stay mad at for long.

As for Patrick, he wants to play house together and make Thanksgiving dinner for their families. But Megan has wept over one failed love and is afraid to risk her heart again.

Wife for Hire

Hank Mallone spotted trouble when she sat down and said she'd marry him. Maggie Toone was a tempting firecracker who'd make his life delightful hell if he let her pretend to be his wife in order to improve his rogue's reputation. Would his harebrained scheme to get a bank loan for his business backfire once Maggie arrived in his small Vermont town and let the gossips take a look?

Maggie never expected her employer to be drop-dead handsome, or to affect her like a belt of bourbon on an empty stomach, but she was too intrigued by his offer to say no . . . and too eager to escape a life that made her feel trapped. The deal was strictly business, both agreed, until Hank turned out to be every fantasy she'd ever had.

Naughty Neighbor

Louisa Brannigan's neighbor was driving her crazy. He snatched her newspaper and listened through her townhouse walls. But when she got fired from her government job, Pete was there, asking her to join his undercover operation. So Louisa was hopelessly entangled—professionally speaking—with the sexiest man alive. Sneaking around corners was fun, especially when the getaway car was a Porsche. Suddenly Louisa was enjoying life on the edge.

Foul Play

When Amy Klasse loses her TV job to a dancing chicken, handsome veterinarian Jake Elliott rescues her with an offer to be his receptionist. Jake just can't resist a damsel in distress, and Amy certainly doesn't mind Jake's charming sincerity.

Then suddenly the job-stealing chicken disappears and Amy is suspected of foul play. Amy and Jake search for clues to prove her innocence. But will Jake be able to prove to Amy that love, too, is a mystery worth solving?

The Grand Finale

Berry Knudsen had a talent for disaster, but when she climbed a tree to rescue a kitten, she wasn't prepared for the scrumptious hunk undressing in a nearby window, or her dive downward that smashed Jake Sawyer's pizza and won his heart! But was there room in her chaotic schedule for a risk-taking inventor with dreams?

Berry took classes, delivered pizzas, and cared for three eccentric old ladies she rescued from the train station. But Jake thrived on a challenge, and he could be very inventive. Could he teach her there was time to make butterscotch pudding and let herself be loved?